THE DAY OF THE DEAD

Caitlin Press Inc.
8100 Alderwood Road, Halfmoon Bay, BC V0N 1Y1
www.caitlin-press.com

Text design by Demian Pettman
Cover design and photo by Vici Johnstone
Printed in Canada

Caitlin Press Inc. acknowledges financial support from the Govern-
ment of Canada and the Canada Council for the Arts, and the Prov-
ince of British Columbia through the British Columbia Arts Council
and the Book Publisher's Tax Credit.

Library and Archives Canada Cataloguing in Publication

Owen, Catherine, author
        The day of the dead : sliver fiction, short stories & an hom-
age/ Catherine Owen.

Issued in print and electronic formats.
ISBN 978-1-987915-20-4 (paperback).--ISBN 978-1-987915-24-2
(ebook)

        I. Title.

PS8579.W43D39 2016   C813'.54   C2016-903266-3
                                               C2016-903267-1

THE DAY OF THE DEAD

sliver fictions, short stories & an homage

Catherine Owen

CAITLIN PRESS

Contents

MEN & WOMEN 1
    360 Degrees 1
    Anthem. 5
    Numb 15
    The Ceremony 19
    A Brief Guide to the Vocabulary of Captors. 20

SIPS: THREE TRUE TALES OF TRAVELLING ALONE AS A WOMAN
IN TURKEY 25
    1. Sultanahmet 25
    2. Taksim Square. 30
    3. Cappadocia 36

THINGS YOU DON'T WANT TO HEAR ABOUT, JOHNNY 41

THE UNSPOKEN SORROW OF THE BLARNEY STONE MAN. . . 42

DOLLFACE 43

SHELF LIFE 45

ALFIE FLIGHT, WELDER & BARD 47

BITE 48

HOLE 56

THE MOUTH. 57

LA ROI DAGOBERT. 58

BOBBLES 59

BREEDERS. 65

THE RESURRECTION. 72

POLLEN 76

FRUITS 77

MUSES 78
   Food I Ate with Frank. 78
   Muse 88
   The Muse-Eaters of Moosonee. 105

THE DEAD 108
   The Man Who Came Back from the Dead 108
   But Not Broken 112
   The Day of the Dead 125
   A Pot of Coffee. 130

A GUY, A GIRL & A GHOST: AN HOMAGE TO MARIE CLAIRE
BLAIS'S THREE TRAVELLERS 132
   Moment One 133
      Sunday 134
      Intermission 137
      Monday. 138
      Montreal. 140
      Monday Night. 142
      Tuesday—Toronto 143
      Tuesday Night 144
      Wednesday—St. James Cathedral 146
   Moment Two 148
      Cantabile e Furioso 148
      Thursday. 149
      Thursday Night. 150
      The Dream 151
   The Final Moment 153
      Friday—Again, the Dream 153
      Friday Night 154
      The Saturday 155

PUBLICATION CREDITS 157

THE AUTHOR 159

For Chris Matzigkeit (1981-2010)
whose loss sings beneath these stories

Men & Women

360 Degrees

"Please, miss, what is this, the name, miss, can you tell me the name?"

How do they know she won't jump up screaming, offended, or even report them to the Coney Island police force for frightening her, for stealing what must surely be a rare insect from the off-season beach, a bug that might have escaped from one of the leftover freak shows at Astroland.

Fortunately for them, she likes to consider herself a kind of amateur entomologist. At home, she has several boxes of insects, dried but unpinned, from June bugs to cockroaches. Although it is more an artistic than a scientific pursuit for her, she does keep a few facts in her head: genus, species, mating habits.

She turns her head slightly, without shifting from her cross-legged position in the sand, to look back to where Caleb is, perched on a stool on the boardwalk, sipping his Labatts.

No, he doesn't seem concerned. More like a little bored with her tendency to run off on him so she can "feel through things without the clutter of another person in the way." But that's the deal. She will vacation with him on the condition that, every day, she can wander away by herself for a while.

At the Brooklyn Bridge, it had been an impulse to zip down to Dumbo to check out that crazy pottery barn while he waited by City Hall for her; in Chelsea, it had been the Miriam Pitt gallery whose showing of Christ figures painted with urine and feces "you just have to see alone to fully appreciate."

And now she is by herself again, at Coney Island, the family fun place, hunched up close to the salt-less tide line, conversing with strange men.

She is asking the two of them where they are from.

"Poland," the old man replies. He wears a toque against the October cold, a blue parka and rubber boots. "But I am American citizen. He is new, visitor, maybe stay."

She takes the other man to be his grandson, about twenty, plush-cheeked, his smile both shy and hungry. He wears similar attire to his grandfather, only he nervously and frequently drags his own toque off his head, dangling it from one bare hand while the other messes with his dark crop of hair.

"Four months," he beams, "four months I here."

She is afraid to tell them what the insect is. Not that she really knows with any certainty.

It's from the genus Mantodea, no doubt about that, like a praying mantis in every way and a female one to boot: shiny green, six thoracic segments, long antennae, folded-up front legs that suggest a penitent, and those alien eyes, so precise in their hunt, capable of swivelling 360 degrees with always that flat, black speck at their centres, watching you with chilly, carnivorous indifference.

But praying mantises are usually four, at most five, inches, and that's the Chinese variety.

The North American ones are smaller, not truly indigenous, having been deposited on these once-wild shores by a cargo ship in 1900.

This creature is at least eight, maybe ten, inches—a miniature dragon.

She is letting it crawl up her arm now and the men are getting nervous.

They had been carrying it about in a takeout container from Nathan's with a plastic bag cinched around the Styrofoam and she had thought it might like some air.

"What are you going to do with it?" she asks them a bit indignantly. "Do you know what it eats?"

"Eat?" the grandfather laughs at her, misunderstanding. "O no, we don't eat it, maybe we eat if we starving, but we in America, right? We not starving!"

She seems to have insulted them. The men exchange a few words in Polish with each other, glancing at her all along. Then the older man becomes more insistent, "Please girl, you just... write the name, write it down."

He shoves an old receipt towards her and the nub of a pencil.

She sighs, letting the delicate, mutated being Morse Code its way down to her fingertips where she unsticks its gluey feet from her skin and slips it back in its sad enclosure.

Then she reaches for the writing materials and, in careful block text, prints: PRAYING MANTIS.

The grandfather looks at the piece of paper, mouthing the syllables to himself, then passes it to the boy so he can knot the plastic bag up again, the creature flailing around in its bubble, a heart hammering within the translucent cavity.

"Ah!" the older man exclaims, taking the paper back and studying it, "praying mantis!"

It is as if she has given him not only a useful but a glorious and astounding tool.

"So praying mantis, it is holy, no?"

Well yes, she thinks to herself, but not in that way.

Instead she says to them, "You two better watch out. The females like to devour their men."

"Oho," the grandfather slaps her on the shoulder while motioning to his grandson to rise, "you are, what do they call them, a ball breaker, yes, good American girl, ho ho."

She watches the two of them teeter off down the beach, the boy's arm slung through the old man's, he carrying the bag between index finger and thumb, the sunlight glowing inside the plastic turning the insect to flint.

Looking around for Caleb, she notices that he had started to walk towards her, perhaps thought better of it, then stopped partway.

Now he is staring at the metallic palm tree, its artificial solitude amid all the grubby sand.

Anthem

It's the emptiness of these beaches that fascinates those from elsewhere. Even at the peak of summer, people are mainly just dots of colour, moving pebbles set against the vastness of blond sand, mazes of driftwood, the Pacific Ocean, the mountains. There might be more See-Doos in July and August, motor boats, but the immensity of water swallows them to near-nothingness, sets the sound of their engines adrift like bees buzzing inconsequentially over the white caps.

Jenny and I come here every summer for a week or so, stay with an artist couple we met at a gallery opening in Vancouver eight years ago. In exchange for errands, sometimes a little modelling work, we can sleep in a converted shed in Hazel and Ted's garden, just steps from the sea.

The year of the foursome I turn thirty-two, choose to celebrate by returning to the coast with Jenny, to further cement our ten-year friendship by reserving this occasion for her particular brand of intimacy: long chats about Derrida, Kristeva and the Beats, reckless laughter over our evening martinis, shared awe for the wild swans at the estuary and the thick pungency of fresh clams.

Hazel and Ted are almost always welcoming, though, at times our spontaneity, our eagerness takes them a little aback. They are getting on in years after all, Hazel's seventy-five, Ted's nearly sixty-eight, and I suppose there comes a point when routine and fixity is more pleasant than rupture or sudden shifts. We sit on their sloping back porch the night of my birthday, the sun's evening rays tapping on the roof.

"Yes, we are getting a bit puttery, aren't we," Hazel comments as she lays down a napkin at each place setting, "but that's still better than doddery, isn't it girls?"

She always calls us girls, no matter how old we are now.

"However you are is fine as long as it's alive," I say to them both, causing Ted to gesture out in the direction of the wood pile.

"On that note, dear, you'll have to see what I've got out there under the tarp. My last exhibit so to speak, a nice rectangular piece in yellow pine." He winks at us, nods sharply towards Hazel.

"Now don't scare the girls," Hazel glances sideways at him, her spidered lips pursing, "that's not for public display yet."

"Really Zell," Jen says, putting the arugula and walnut salad on the picnic table, "we're a bit too grownup to spook that easily."

"O I suppose," Hazel admits, stretching one turpentine-scented hand towards the bread basket, "but I just don't like to put a damper on things. It's Rosemary's party after all. Ted, dear, why don't you open that nice pinot blanc that Justin brought us?"

φ

Gallery Sachet is where Jenny and I met them. One of those drizzly East Van afternoons where graffiti seems to run down the cheeks of the buildings like unlawful mascara. When we were both in university, I'd often study on weekend mornings at Calabria, poring over Butler and Irigaray while inhaling multiple shot glasses of espresso. After lunching on a brioche or panini, I'd jitter with my book-swollen knapsack down the Drive to rendezvous with Jen at one cultural event or another. There were so many in those days: poetry readings, community open stages, micro-theatre companies showing *Waiting for Godot* or *Major Barbara*, and gallery openings. We went partially

6

for the thrill of complimentary mid-day wine, but also to glimpse whatever it was they were currently hanging. Some installation work, usually. Giant balloons full of blood, a video of a man chopping wood on a downtown median, a naked woman dancing to Bolero while pulling handkerchiefs, in all colours, out of her cunt.

These were good to theorize to later, over a stack of fries at Fets. You know, how was the woodsman expressing a state of post-colonial hybridity, the kerchief girl embodying a feminist jouissance enclosed in the patriarchal object?

But by the time we met Hazel and Ted we were both nearly finished our master's and had wearied of such conjecturing.

"God don't you just want to be quiet for a while, no words at all, anywhere, only some beautiful thing in front of you that silences the mind!"

That's Jen, on our way to Gallery Sachet and then, there it was.

One of Ted's masks, then another and a third, emerging like dream faces from the white, grain shining, features curved into the most miraculous expressions.

"Like looks you never see on your own face, because, well, you're so absorbed in the moment!" I stuttered out after an endless hush. "Like cumming or this horrendous grief, or when you were a child and first felt awe just knowing you were alive."

Ted, I later realized, had been listening to my outburst from a short distance away, the plastic demitasse of wine pinched like a flower stem in his callused fingers, but he didn't speak to us until we'd moved onto Hazel's part of the exhibit, paintings, strange and wondrous, of the insides of mechanical things: blenders, grinders, a wind-up clock, captured as if they were as transient and fragile as O'Keeffe's blooms.

"Isn't she marvellous!" Ted leaned into us, the work, nodding his powerful head, smiling.

"Do you know her?" Jen asked, staring up into a face that was mostly the rich growth of beard.

"That I do and well, as a matter of fact. I'm the mask maker man."

"O you're married to her!"

"Close as it gets, yes, been living with the champ about forty years now."

"We love your work, both your work I mean, it's just, well, we so needed beauty today, that's Jen, I'm Rosemary, Rose, and yours was the first real beauty we saw. I feel broken open right now, to tell you the truth."

"Not a bad thing dears, is it? You know Kafka once had something to say about that, but here, let me introduce you to Hazel."

And so it began.

φ

Neither of them wants to join us at the pub.

"O no girls, you go ahead, the fogeys like their nightcaps and the CBC about this time, you know us."

"But it's Rose's birthday!" Jen protests.

"All the better to celebrate it then, there's times when youth should stick to youth, don't you think, Ted?"

Ted is clearing up the plates, wiping down the wooden table.

"Humph, what's that?"

"The girls should head to The Shoreline alone, wouldn't you say?"

"God yes, that place is a cesspool for minnows with the faces of ghouls and the beer is flat!"

"It's not so bad, Ted," Jen elbows him as he passes her on the way to the kitchen, "you're exaggerating as usual."

"Well, what if I am, the point is, that place is not the business of a couple of creepy-crawlers like ourselves at 10 pm, now go, have some drinks, find yourselves a few lads to chat with, but beware, such shilly-shallying can lead to forty years of shack-up."

Hazel smiles at him, "Put the kettle on then love and let's leave these two revellers til the morning."

Ted gives us the brusque salute he always does before turning in while Hazel squeezes our shoulders affectionately and then it's just Jen and me and the fizzing of the sea beyond their gate.

φ

The Shoreline or, as I used to call it, the "Heard that line" pub, is about a quarter of a mile from Hazel and Ted's, a modified log cabin suspended on enormous pylons over the ocean. It serves the typical: fish and chips, chowder, burgers. Bar's open until midnight.

Jen and I find a choice spot on the deck; the place is nearly empty, even the sound system's on low. Tide is high though, and salty kelp smells rise to hit us along with the buzz we get too quickly from our Strongbows.

"How will we survive them dying?" I say to no one in particular, looking around the quiet room through the wide panes of glass on one side of the deck. "Who hoo, thirty-two and life just keeps getting wilder!"

Jen seems agitated, antsy as she gets when life isn't moving fast enough for her.

"Let's get some Sambucas shall we, old lady?"

Jen loves that cloudy sup of liquorice, the clink of those tough little glasses, the shudder that rips down her spine afterwards. "C'mon, I'm buying. We'll make our own party won't we."

"As always," I laugh, downing the last of my cider.

φ

We see the boys jogging down the island highway by the pub around 11:30. Even in the dark, we know they are young, lean, excitable, foreign.

"Wow." I slur. "Makes me feel old and crabby."

"Whatever Rose," Jen's voice flows around me. I can barely see her mouth anymore.

"Look—two of them are coming in—lil cuties!"

The only other people in the bar at this point are a couple, middle-aged, dressed in western garb and a sullen looking twenty-something in a mac jacket. The boys briefly scan the room, easily settling on us.

"Hey, they're coming over, lookie!"

"Yeah, big surprise huh. Now don't go telling them how old I am, ya hear?"

Drinking makes me lose the desire for truth, replacing it with an ache for adventure, illusion.

"Hi girls, I am Benuto, this is Luis, we are from Mexico, you mind we join you?"

"Vacationing?" Jen stretches her arm across the table as they sit down, plonking her hand heavily on the place mat as if she's serving the Grand Slam breakfast.

"Yes, but also we learn English."

"Here on the island?"

"O no, in Vancouver, here we come for trip, weekend trip, stay in over there." Rodrigo points to a row of apartments across from the beach. "Nine of us."

"Nine, eh," I finally venture. "Why don't they come over too, more the merrier."

"No, they too young. Only Luis and I we are nineteen, they seventeen, eighteen."

Benuto is the voluable one, white-toothed, gelled locks. Luis barely speaks, his curly hair draping his eyes, a silver cross around his neck.

The bar is about to close. Benuto flashes a tiny flask he takes from his pocket, says, "We go for a walk, ladies?"

Leaving the pub, we quickly pair off, I with the taciturn Luis while Jen gabs on with Benuto, grabbing his hand as she leads him downstairs to the chilled waterfront.

"Let's go swimming, Rose. We're tough, right, we're tough?"

"Yeah, naked?"

"Course. We're BC chicks, aren't we?"

So we rip off our capris and tee-shirts, the boys throwing themselves down on logs, laughing at us.

"You girls crazy. Too cold, too cold!"

But we are already bare and dashing towards the black waves.

While we splash about in the kelp-strung surf, Benuto begins to sing, a rich, mocking tune.

"What's he singing?" I gurgle to Jen.

"Listen babes. It's about ush, haha, ush."

His notes carry over the stretch of beach between us like night birds.

"I love Canadian girls, because they are so beautiful," he sings over and over again.

"O god. What is beauty anyway," I begin but Jen shushes me.

"No analysis you. It's your birthday and they want us. Those baby men want our bodies. Yippee yip," she yodels, shaking her breasts from side to side, spraying me.

Suddenly we see a flash, then another.

"They're taking pictures of ush. Stop doing that!"

"O whatever. So we get our photos in their ESL albums and become beeg stars in Mexico."

"Well I care!" I begin running towards the boys, Jen chasing me, screaming, "whoop, whoop!" sand clothing our feet, calves, Benuto snapping, singing, even Luis trying to grin.

Then I have the camera in my wet hand and am flinging it down between the logs.

"I love Canadian girls, because they are soooooooooo beautiful," Benuto sings in my face, slapping my damp ass cheeks, flipping me over.

His cock is hard and inside me fast, only a few minutes, Jen and Luis looking on, suddenly still, before he says, "O sorry man, this one yours, no?" sliding out of me and sticking himself in Jen from behind, still humming his tune of praise, reduction.

Luis is clearly not as skilled at seducing anyone and the Sambuca is wearing off by then, so I try to start a conversation instead.

"So what do you like to do, when you're not studying?"

He's still scarcely looked at me. Curls mingling with lashes.

"Write."

"Well, that's good. Jen and I write a lot."

"Really?" He brightens. "What write?"

"Papers, poems, for work, manuals, brochures, stuff like that, boring."

"I write stories."

Out of the corner of my eye I can see the shadow of Benuto's cock sliding in and out of Jen. She is bent over, fingers digging into loosening bits of bark.

"Hey man, hurry up you," Benuto calls over as he keeps thrusting. "I be done soon and then I want more, so you go Luis, you go!"

"Do you want to do this?" he asks me, as if we are undertaking something very daring, life-altering.

Knowing his status with Benuto will be compromised if I resist, not wanting Jen to have the only experience of the evening and then too, feeling that vague lust I always do towards strangers, I tell him, "It can be good for your stories and anyway, it's my birthday."

"Nice," he replies as I mount him, his prick slender, almost feminine, he clenching his eyes shut to cum as Benuto bellows, "O Canadian girls!" spraying his load over Jen's back, all sparkles of salt and moonlight.

φ

"And how did those shenanigans go last night?" Ted is frying up bacon, brewing espressos, as Jen and I stumble into the kitchen late the next morning, Hazel sitting on the floral couch in the sunroom, reading the paper and stroking one of their plush, ornery cats.

How bright the room is, purring, Chopin on low in the background.

"O god—" is all I can venture.

"Was it worth it?" Hazel laughs.

Jen has slumped into one of the bamboo chairs, her hand slathered over her forehead.

"Can't believe we have to bus back today. Whose idea was that?"

"No men hiding out in the shed you're smuggling back in your bags?"

"None of that now, Ted. You know the girls aren't tarts."

"No, no, but they want to get hooked up like the rest of us. I mean look at all we have, Ms. Hazel, who wouldn't want that?"

Jen groans at this and I think about Benuto's song, its silly homage echoing over those vacant beaches, Luis's emptiness, the way we'd fucked like machines with parts missing, the mask of my drunken, unlovely face he would carry back with him to the hot crowds of Mexico, my white flesh a speck in the lens, a stone.

Numb

But what if she hadn't felt anything then, even then?

That's really, when she thinks about it, what worries Zita.

Andrew is sitting up in bed, hair crumpled up like the draft of a bad poem, smoking, staring at Zita from time to time with the weariness of a primordial creature.

"It's because of all you've been through that you want... that."

"You think so?"

"Well obviously. No real rocket science there. Cause and effect."

She isn't so sure. Maybe that's just the way she's always been, the way she's put together, a watcher on the edges of horror, pleasure, whatever, and now she simply has an alibi, an excuse for the men in her life to rest their sense of inadequacy on like an IKEA pillow, uncomfortable, reassuringly bright.

"Tea and cereal, a movie?"

Andrew's voice has lightened. They have had the talk again. He has obviously attained a satisfying conclusion and now, by placing the familiar stamp of routine on their interchange, can look on Zita once more with what, in a man's mind at least, passes for love.

φ

Zita has been told by sundry lovers over the years that she clings to morbid fascinations. What this means, she has deduced, above and beyond the dead things she keeps in her freezer: a mouse stiffened into a moon shape, a sparrow her cat got, even past the beaver, turtle and cow skulls she keeps on her bookcases, and the piece of art she's been working on for years—images of junkies shooting up set in dipty-ches with slabs of raw meat—is her elusiveness.

Her lovers know she is preoccupied, always, with some-thing outside of their living bodies. Such distractedness defines her morbidity for them—as if she were always listening for ghosts, voices from the spirit world, things un-fleshed.

Has Zita always been like this though, a rare glass ornament as she likes to think of herself, opaque and un-shatterable, yet so finely blown that she holds the light in unforgiveable proportions?

Or is Zita, in fact, defective, as so many of them have raged at her while scrabbling on the floor for their clothes before slamming out into the night and its silences.

Either interpretation can be readily drawn, dependent on whether one is enchanted or disillusioned.

Andrew has stuck around for a while though.

He wants to get to the bottom of it.

φ

On Sundays, Andrew and Zita take their bikes down to the river.

Even when it is below zero, they ride, muscles blooming beneath Gore-Tex and fleece.

The river with all its mouths of ice still flowing.

φ

What it comes down to, Zita thinks, is that Andrew likes a good mystery. Likes things that are initially complex to reveal themselves, eventually, as only tidy formulas.

Weekdays, he drives a truck. On Saturdays sometimes he'll help people he knows move house, people who pay in pizza, Pilsners. For an abstract kind of satisfaction more than anything, the weird thrill he gets of fitting their domestic fragments together in his vehicle: bookcase alongside couch, entertainment unit by end table, a solid puzzle of angles.

"Physics is what it is," Andrew likes to crow after the job's done, when he's back home with Zita, scorfing down the noodles she's boiled up for him with hoisin, sesame seeds.

"Everything's really just a math problem."

"Even love?" Zita just has to prod him, though what love is or isn't scarcely ever concerns her.

"O yeah. That too," Andrew plonks his tumbler of Beaujolais down like a gavel. "A mere equation when it comes down to it, a biological adding game."

"Well!" Zita feigns shock. "And you call me frigid."

ϕ

Not that Andrew has ever used that word, its silly Freudian syllables conjuring up a scraped-back bun, spectacles, primly folded hands, a dimity blouse.

After all, Zita has had lots of sex.

ϕ

The first time, Zita was thirteen.

The boy took her to his house.

His father was mowing the lawn, wearing only a cowboy hat and shorts with the American flag on them.

When the boy stuck it inside Zita, she was listening to the sound of the motor as it rowed its long lines through the summer grasses, and when he came she was water for a moment.

Then she noticed that the boy was now wearing her lipstick, the frosty pink glisten transferred to him through all those little pre-emptory kisses he had bestowed on her.

They were the same person, Zita decided. Zita One and Zita Two.

Therefore, she had to conclude, nothing had happened.

Zita bought liquorice on the way back to the bus stop, ropy, red and sweet.

φ

Andrew is under the covers again. Andrew is between her legs. He doesn't give up easily, Zita thinks.

They have been living together for nineteen months now.

"Bite me!" Zita hears herself saying. "Tie me up dammit!"

Andrew has learned to ignore her by now. He loves Zita, he says. He doesn't want to hurt her.

His tongue persists in its slow damp circlings. Andrew will teach her how to feel he says. Zita is his project.

But if Zita's always been like this, then there's no breaking through all the damage of the past, no chance of that victory cry erupting from the gentle battle Andrew is having with her flesh.

She was so flat at thirteen, she remembers, that her and the boy's chests squeaked together, popping and farting sweatily as he moved inside her. They were only machines then, already gone wrong.

The Ceremony

Thirty-one, and Shanni is the only white woman on the grounds of the Kofuku-ji Temple, unmarried, again. On the lam from quiche lorraine, RRSPs and a Pekingese named Rufous.

The second Monday in January and a thousand girls clad in lush furisode kimonos, waists fluted by obis, are giggling down the gracious path to Kasugu shrine.

She doesn't know what she is doing here, stuffing all this youth into her eyes.

At twenty, she had already been shacked up, she and Ray wed by a JP at Da Mario's where they had later gorged on gnocchi. By twenty-two it was splitsville following a miscarriage and one too many screwdrivers.

"Silly thing," her mother's usual tact. "What else did you expect?"

Well, she hadn't had those sleeves for one, generous silky expanses surging down over un-ringed fingers, pricy signs of being single. "As much as car," a beamy-eyed man says to her, pointing in the direction of what must be his daughter, lifting the camera to his face heavily, memory a fluid that could spill, like oil, like tears.

She'd only had the casual slide into what passed for Canadian adulthood.

No elders at the shiki lecturing about responsible citizenship.

No priestly archers extolling the techniques of marital bull's eye.

These girls know what comes next.

Beneath their giddy lustre, a calm has already shaped itself, ponderous and sombre as the deer of Nara Park, those divine messengers of the gods, antlers curved in such precise forms of yielding.

A Brief Guide to the Vocabulary of Captors

The man from Zeballos hands out tomatoes. Where the hell is Xanadu, she wonders. The Greyhound marquee slides through the S's: Smile, Slave Lake, Smithers, School-bus, past the V's: Vancouver, Vernon, then stops at the only available X name.

Isn't that in Africa?

The man, lanky, sandy, on his way to work for BC Hydro's dam in the mostly-Native enclave, miles through the bush past Union Bay, extends the Tupperware towards her again.

Cherry tomatoes toss about like pinballs.

She takes some. She isn't proud.

"Take some more. Have as many as you like," he says. "Fact is, me and Anne are sick of them. Grow them in Kamloops. A bright little garden I get to see once every two weeks or so. Yup, two on, two off for the most part."

"Don't you get tired of it?" she wonders.

"Course. Been doing it for a year and a half now, but it's bound to end soon. Then I'll be sent somewhere else. Like the freedom most days."

He briefly appraises her like a favourable crop.

"Hey, you look like quite the free spirit yourself."

His name is Jan, pronounced the Danish way. Jan from Denmark. Originally that is. He was only four when he left. What could have led him to consider her a free spirit? Perhaps her backpack, only three-quarters full, its main pocket marked by a poorly sewn on patch of a Canadian flag; the braids that dangle from beneath her cap; the relaxed patter with which she chats to him, calm as if she weren't suddenly homeless.

She often gave off this impression to strangers—a silly young thing, footloose, a bit easy. It is one of her most convenient masks. Wouldn't do to tell Jan she is fleeing.

φ

"Zeballos was named after a Spanish officer. Didn't discover the damn place of course. He just stopped off long enough to stamp his foreign mark on it. The Nuu-chah-nulth people were there long before him needless to say."

"No places named after women," she interjects, a statement that her Women's History classes at UBC had taught her to insert into almost every historical discussion. It has become a mechanical response now, contextualizing absence.

He draws in his breath at that, sighs, unfurling his legs beneath the seat in front of him, clasping his freckled hands in his lap.

"Hmmm. Nope, none that I can think of." A silence, as though he is wondering whether to pursue this trajectory then, "So you were mentioning a partner? That's a coincidence indeed. I have a partner too. Won't be tied down will we. She wants to hook up more permanently, but it's just never been my thing, the whole formal religious stuff. What's it all mean anyhow, Haley?"

She shrugs, wondering why she has told him her name, why he won't stop talking to her.

They are on the ferry now, just rocking away from the dock, the ship's whistle is about to blow, those on the outside deck should cover their ears.

φ

She had been caught. That was what had happened. Perhaps not so unbelievably considering the fatalism with which she had always undertaken affairs, not bothering to delete emails, hide pictures, or prevent daydreams from spoiling the domestic routine.

In fact, everything she had done in the last week had been an acceleration of such carelessness, clearly pointing to a desire to be stopped, to have the narrative she had been living, with all its secret antagonists and cramped plot twists, drawn to a swift conclusion.

The final scenario she had concocted, in which her last overly young lover had been reeled into an embrace between the toaster oven and garburator while her partner lay in the next room, vodka-weakened but still within simple ear shot of their moans, had brought all to a relatively conclusive end.

"Out!" he had growled at them both, stumbling towards them in his velour dressing gown, the tiny silver hatchet they had used on camping trips in hand and she had gone. Not with her lover of course, who she had only liked for his nipple rings and moony eyes. By herself. Leaving their bungalow in Richmond, heading for the coast.

It is pointless to wonder now whether another, more delicately wrought form of closure wasn't possible, even preferable.

Her stories all seemed to end with her rather graceless departure.

"You read a lot, don't you," Jan is saying to her between bites of a Triple O special from the West Coast Café. "Well, I'll tell you about the best book I've read in a long time. *The White Slaves of Nootka*. All about Zeballos when it was ruled by Chief Maquinna. There were many Chief Maquinnas actually. Name means something like possessor of pebbles."

She decides to feign interest.

"Pebbles as in currency? Why pebbles?"

"Got me there, Haley, could'a been that I suppose, more useful than they are today, pebbles. But anyway, this book is about the Maquinna who ruled around 1801, '02, around there, told by Mr. John R. Jewitt, one of old Maquinna's slaves, a white guy no less, caught after the massacre of the *Boston*, his ship. Crazy, eh?"

They are on the evening ferry. Through the glass she glimpses the furred shape of the moon, the reflections of lines of bulbs, shuddering along with the engine. She has been trying to read *Serenissima*, by Ray Smith, that tragedy of an aging coquette's flounder breasts, cruelly revealed by the predatory ingenue in her blood-red dress. And the end in a bar, paying young boys for sex over a toilet seat, all her lingerie shredded. "What others called promiscuity was in fact love, a fullness of love spilling out of her," Smith wrote and as much as she clings to that line a horror still squats in her mind of turning out like that. Albeit less romantically, in a non-Venetian setting. That desperate, one of those floating old women grasping at smooth flesh like a mirage of silks.

Not that she is old yet. Mid-thirties. Not old. But she can see the pattern now, the sequences of commitments interspersed by dark dashes of seduction, a sick Morse Code that signals the same thing over and over again. Her life a suffocating little hive and herself the doyenne of all those cells.

φ

"Please return to your vehicles..." the woman's voice unpeels itself through the loudspeaker, as inevitable as if she is announcing, "and so they lived happily ever after."

Jan is stuffing his wrappers into the bin's perfectly round mouth, still blatting away at her, "So you want to know how our John fellow survived?"

"Sure." She peers out the window to where the lights of Nanaimo are tightening at their approach, the next crew already clotting at the dock, waiting to take over the sailing.

"You see, the trick was, he learned the Natives' language, got a decent vocabulary going, so he could know what mattered to those people and that way, he came to be respected, almost one of them. Saved his hide anyway. Smart guy."

She nods as she follows him down to Deck 4 where their Greyhound is parked, the driver bald and solicitous, one of the passengers hanging out by the door, talking about last week's fatal bus stabbing, "They say the guy was looking at his woman, no? I mean what else is a man to do."

Sips: Three True Tales of Travelling Alone as a Woman in Turkey

1. Sultanahmet

Buying a gift for your lover's wife requires a certain indelicacy of conscience, but I am determined to do so anyway. After all, I am visiting Turkey, the land of their birth, mainly to uncover things about my lover impossible in a Canadian context. This is a trip that requires a kind of propitiation. Thus far, I've only sensed what an anomaly he is, this chilled, taciturn man, proudly ineffable. So different from the men on every corner with their overheated invitations. "Hey lady, sexy girl, be my wife! Marry me! Want to come home?" However, I also know I must be missing something, having only been in Sultanahmet twenty-four hours, the majority of them spent in the hostel, The Daffodil, smoking peach shisha from a hookah and munching hard-boiled eggs in the top floor lounge overlooking the dangerous sea.

The owner, Mahsoud, warned me away from the docks, told me the Sufi dancers weren't worth the ticket price and even that I should watch out for the crooked vendors at the many shish kebab stands.

They overcharge, especially they see pretty white girl and they think things, you alone, why?

I can't explain this to them. The reason I have travelled halfway across the world by myself. Such a trip only marks me as wealthy, slutty in their eyes and no amount of further narrative detail serves to humanize me beyond this serviceable stereotype. So I've been held a kind of hostage at a corner table in the hostel lounge, a room of blue walls, posters of Rumi and Cappadocia. As the hours pass, I read Kerouac and watch the parched quickness of lizards slipping in and out of the rusted roof tiles, wondering how to release myself from Mahsoud's dictates without risking my life when he says to me, poking his head around the top of the stairs, *You, me, we go for a walkabout, visit my uncle, he be happy, I introduce you?*

I have become weary enough of my surroundings that I am determined to believe him a safe option. Two days and already I am feeling the desperation of the ultra-visible, a constant sense of exposure every time I venture out that has distracted me from why I am here. Perhaps with a man at my side, a business owner, I will diminish to controlled, shadowy proportions again and thus free up some mental space to think of my lover, his wife, how this folie à trois had all unfolded.

However, Mahsoud keeps trying to take me by the hand as we stroll past the tour bus ringed environs of Hagia Sofia, the less popular gate to the sewers, the oldest hammam in Turkey from which steam, the pile of soft white towels, a glisten of heated flesh, wafts. I am unable to let the armour that has settled on me loosen for a moment, men's eyes now following the luck of my chaperone, a homely man who has apparently snagged a white tourist girl.

Hayir. I smile tightly at him, refusing to grab his hand, testing out one of the few Turkish words I have learned. *Pardon.*

But why?

Don't... want a boyfriend.

O.

Mahsoud seems perplexed, chastened, lets his fingers fall against the slippery fabric of his chinos, *My uncle here, him. Come.*

He nods towards a stolid man in an Armani suit, a full head of salt hair, standing in front of the sign for Karim's Persian Carpets, fine importers and distributors. He is smoking a cigar but when he spies Mahsoud, his mouth opens in a blank startle of teeth.

I suddenly feel like a fly drawn by the promise of light, air, into the gluey mesh that passes for family in this tourist town, all relatives doubling as traders, dealers, traps. Mr. K, as he calls himself, purrs towards me, *Please my dear, like cousins no?* as he leads me and Mahsoud into the brightly lit showroom, then downstairs, to a corner with a couch, ornate chairs, motioning to his salesgirl to fetch us drinks.

Coffee, tea, apple tea, what do you prefer my dear? His English is perfect, hardened into a shiny patter.

O, apple tea, why not, I sigh. (Only later will I come to comprehend the soporific, lulling qualities of this beverage when I finally escape Sultanahmet for a tour of Cappadocia. Every stop our little troop of tourists is taken to: the rug factory, a pottery barn, the glassware manufacturers, we are plied with apple tea prior to the inevitable sales pitch.)

Almost instantly, the girl returns with a tray on which sit three narrow mugs of apple tea, a few sweet biscuits, placing them on the long teak table in front of the couch where Karim has suggested we sit.

Mahsoud here, my nephew, he is a fine young business man, is he not my lady? A real catch as they say. Unfortunately, his English skills are not yet superior. But then he doesn't spend half the year in New York as his uncle does.

His finely clipped, well-polished hand comes to a landing on my knee, *Having fun with the men, my dear?*

I shift forward to take a sip of the false orchard in my cup.

That's not why I'm here actually, more a research trip.

O but young ladies like yourself, hot, special, surely…

Mahsoud seems to lean into the lascivious tone, wetting his plush lips as Mr. K grins at me as though they share a velvet secret.

It's important to relax, no? I myself have a wife but when I'm away, ahhhhh, I find my pleasures, a girlfriend here, there, sex relaxation is good for the body, no guilt, guilt is no good my dear.

I think briefly of my lover's lean flesh, of his long, entangled hair, fingers he always wants me to suck, right down to the webbing between the digits. There is nothing relaxing about being with him though. My body always tenses up at his touch, becomes hard, highly strung. My cries of pleasure sharp, hacking sounds he always hushes, afraid of his wife hearing them, even when she is out of town, far away.

Can I see some carpets? I ask, suddenly deciding that the only way to reclaim this unwanted visit to a rug merchant in the guise of family, this undesired overture by a hostel owner under the auspices of a friendly stroll, is to buy my lover's wife a gift here. Yes, I will bring her back a rug, something opulent, a soft gesture of unsaid apology for having fallen in love with, become addicted to in a sense, her elusive, difficult, hypnotic husband.

Mr. K gleams as if I have provided him proof, once again, of the gold lying beneath his charm, patting my thigh. Then he waves his hand towards a boy who has dipped out of what must be the storeroom.

Bring them to the lady, Hasif, all of them.

Mahsoud slips upstairs, to get his cut, I am sure, his work as an intermediary accomplished, while I take over an hour to select a circular rug, blue and rose, woven with the traditional symbol for Ararat on it, a bold triangle clasped by a vise of mysterious patterns. So many carpets had flown around me, mesmeric, spinning like heavy butterflies from the boy's slight hand, all those tightly packed threads, dyes of berries, charcoal, oyster shells, symbols of women, of water, the scarab beetle, the pomegranate. Each rug containing its own unique flaw, deliberately introduced into the weft to humanize its design.

Ararat is a good choice my dear, a lucky one, comments Mr. K as he signs the bill of sale, hand curving over my shoulder, a chaste, fatherly grip now he has been given my credit card number. *It is, after all, where the ark landed at the end of those forty days and nights of flood. And everything that had entered two by two, as it should be, came out, my lady, saved.*

2. Taksim Square

Looking at Emre, short but concealing a muscled arsenal beneath that button-down shirt, the scent of a practised seducer despite his sloping pupil, an eye lazy as egg white in his face, I am caught between anxiety and the curiosity bred in me from years of being a writer. It's raining or I never would have come here. Not just drizzling (I am after all a Vancouverite and can handle showers with equanimity) but a torrent of wet that slashes the surface of the Bosphorus, driving the bridge fishers home, that cascades over Taksim Square's marquees and the endless blatting of horns. Simit Saraya is about to close. It is 3 am. I had just arrived in the city earlier that day to a miscommunication. One contact had thought the other one was picking me up, as I discovered much later, and so I had been left stranded, straying about the square. At first, content to play gypsy, I spent several hours at a restaurant eating Greek salad and thick wedges of buttery bread, watching the garishly energetic street life, but as it grew dark, worry began to jab. After walking around in circles for some time, I came upon this late night Internet café and plonked my backpack down for the duration. Now though, they are closing. "Excuse me, miss, but shut now," the young boy peers sideways at me where I sit scrawling in my journal. "Do you know where I can go to sleep?" I ask him. "Hotel?" he offers but I already know that, in this area of town, hotels range upwards of 300 euros a night, my entire budget for this two-week trip. He has no other suggestions.

So I toss down the last of my Nescafé, crumple up the wax paper that clenches one of their pasty buns, crammed with cheese or spinach or jam, heft the damp bag on my shoulder again and push open the door. Once, years ago when I was still in my twenties, on the trail of a poem, I had bedded down in a Clark Drive squat, if bedded you could call it as all they were offering was a mat, scrawny blankets, one candle and a night of junkie prowlings, for bicycle wheels, syringes, chocolate milk, the kid called Blake constantly telling me to "Chilloutchilloutchillout!" The experience had given me the sense that I can, if needed, tough things through, which I obviously have no choice but to do now, plumping my jacket beneath my head, just under the partial covering of an awning outside the dark café. Four hours until dawn.

"Up, up! Out!" Someone is shaking my arm, yanking at it. I must have fallen asleep for a few minutes. A policeman tugs at my sleeve, pointing for me to get up, move along. *"Kanadoleum"* is all I think to gasp in my approximate Turkish, as if a northern status condones me dossing down on the pavement. Here, people call Canada "that cold heaven" my Turkish friends had told me before I left. Those few days ago how androgynous and innocent I had felt, planning to conquer everything, to overcome so much. I hadn't known then that, as a woman alone, I am viewed only as easy, rich. Justifying, from them, a certain combination of disdain and hunger. The policeman however doesn't care that I am Canadian, a woman, he merely wants me to keep going, no other interest in my well-being. He is only concerned, as must be the case in the vacuity of all big cities, that tourists not witness vagabonds. I rise with difficulty, start to walk. How could there be that many cats in this city, everywhere, clinging like *kargas* to drainpipes, the cusps of roofs, skirting the traffic circle, nursing their perilous babies beneath the giant letters of the Levi's sign. My bag is heavy with wet. My feet scrape the pavement as I dawdle towards the core of the square, almost too tired to wonder what I will do next.

And then Emre appears, beckoning me from a doorway in that deceptive haven of English—"Excuse me, miss, but do you need some help?" It is my lover Hasan's fault in a sense, I realize again, the reason I am here, for being so different—his slowed beauty, sullen shyness, impossibly quiet longings have failed to prepare me for the more regular gregariousness, crude flirtations and, harder, the insistence masquerading as hospitality. My adolescent fling with a Serb might have allowed me to intuit this, the parents pushing all manner of things from homemade wine to an antique wedding ring on me. I from a Puritan upbringing, where one serving should always be sufficient, had been shocked. But this was long ago. How was I to know the exception is not the norm? Yes, I am cold, tired and drenched. The rain unceasing.

"Nowhere is open anymore to get *kahva* or even *su*," he remarks as if casually, strolling beside me, a proffered umbrella floating above our heads. "I have a place though, comfortable, small, but you can sleep, promise, a pleasure to assist a Canadian, really." Yes I have told him where I come from, about the miscommunication. My national pride rises, sewn as tightly inside me as the patch is on my pack, and I relent.

Now I look more closely at him. In his apartment, a brisk fifteen-minute stroll away from Taksim. His suite is not tastefully furnished. A shoe rack in the front hall of the three-storey walk-up, narrow sofa in the den, a stack of videos—*Barbarella, When Harry Met Sally*—in the sole bookcase. The only knick-knacks I see are a set of Babushkas, usually slipped one within the other, but here placed in order of ascending height on a whitewashed shelf.

"O a girlfriend gave me those," he tells me, catching my gaze. "A Russian. She lived with me awhile."

It is only long after, staying with the lawyer from Be-yoglu who takes pity on me, a girl without a place to stay, nearly broke, that I hear of The Natashas, a name that con-jures up a cheesy girl group but refers to sex slaves from the steppes, blonde-haired women lured to Turkey by work, kept, sometimes as long as ten years, before their bodies are found. If I'd only known this story before, I would have choked up my food allowance for a room, my traveller's cheapness be damned. Instead, my friends back home had only cautioned me to watch my drinks at bars, keep ID on me at all times. And so I pay attention as, in the box of his kitchen, Emre pours us tea, hot water slamming over the rim of pale mugs, the tea bags, cinnamon peach, bobbing on top. "Cookies?" he asks, still playing my saviour.

I sit beside him on the couch and sip as though I am sucking up tiny slivers. He won't stop staring at me. "I'm so tired," I begin.

"O I know," he replies cryptically.

"Really, I must sleep after this."

"We have a bed, we do. You can sleep alone. Promise," he repeats. Jumping up, opening a closet door, he pulls out a sheet and tosses it on the carpet like an affirmation, "You see, I will sleep here."

How badly I want to feel secure. To imagine actually being able to rest in this strange man's place. But I know this is impossible, dangerous.

And even now he is gawping at me again oddly with his shifty sluggish eye, "You are crazy, no? To come to a stranger's house?"

"Well," I play the naïve Canadian of folklore, "back at home we have no locks on our doors. Everyone is to be trusted. In Canada."

"Really? What a bonus place to live! How do you like my English. It's good yes?"

I agree. Very good actually. But how? I want to ask him how he learned it, where he's from but he is saying to me in a harder tone, "You must shower now. Shower before bed. Get clean." He opens the closet again, takes out a pair of folded grey pajamas, shoves them towards me, "Shower, then change into these."

My hand automatically slides to my midsection to check my money belt in which there is lira, a passport. I try for a smile around my rising ire, "O no, I couldn't. So sleepy. Just need that bed." But now his features have suddenly seized into a simmer on the edge of frightening, "But you will make me angry. I am trying to be kind. Come now. I insist." His sharp arms are urging me towards the stark bathroom where he turns on the shower, tests the heat, "See. This feels nice. Just relax. Get clean now." Then he leaves me there. The door doesn't lock. I stand by the spray awhile, the water draining down, clutching the institutional nightwear, certain there is no way I will get naked, not willingly.

A year before this trip, I had first stripped in front of Hasan. "I want to see you," he had nearly whispered, gazing at me from the couch as, slightly disgraced, I had stood, sticking out the small points of my breasts, cupping my pudenda, lusting for him wholly yet incapable of acting. Finally I had moved towards his belt, as though asleep in my desire, releasing his cock and taking it between my lips while he hardly shifted, barely moaned, a contained hunger I could never fathom, never stir him beyond.

I exit the barren square of the bathroom, decline once more, phrasing my refusal carefully, afraid of incurring threats, "It's simply not my country's custom," I strain towards a cliché of womanhood, "In Canada, women don't shower at stranger's houses. Not about trust. About, um, shyness, modesty. So can you show me where I can sleep?"

He had been staring out the window, a plot of darkness in the wall, facing nothing. He is not to be fooled that easily. "But crazy girls from Canada go to stranger's houses?" he remarks, a sour ridicule in his words. He doesn't insist though, gesturing instead towards the bedroom, "Sleep in there. On top of the sheets. You are too dirty. I'll be out here then." I peer in, enter. The room is white and red. Teddy bears are strewn on every available surface and the satin duvet is quilted with *Sene Sevyorum*—"I love you." What kind of a grown man's bedroom is this? A sudden hunkering down of nausea in me, the ache to flee, even if it means throwing myself out the window. Of course I won't rest here, in this creepy saccharine room, would have been better walking the streets. Still, I am anxious about angering him so lie down, hug myself to protect my money, identity, wondering how much longer I have to wait until it's light. Minutes later, from what seems a great distance, I hear the door swish open over the too-thick pile of carpet and then Emre climbs in beside me, grows against me in the dark.

3. Cappadocia

The hammam on the edge of Goreme displays all the pretensions of being ancient: clay walls, a massive stone dais, cracked mosaic tiles on the floor. In fact, it had been built late last year and only opened six months ago, according to the brochure I am perusing in the lobby while waiting to be escorted up to the change rooms. "Distressed." The word pops into my mind unbidden. Is that not what my lover does back in Vancouver? Distress furniture, coarsening its grain with steel wool and sandpaper, fretting away paint until the bookcase or table looks like a French chateau find? This hammam, I notice, is full of distressed textures, beautiful scars glowing in the melting light.

Only the receptionist speaks English, sufficient English at any rate to take my twenty-five euros for this "invigorating, traditional experience" as the brochure promises. I have been in the Cappadocia region for three days now. On Sunday, I boarded the all-night bus from the Beyoglu district of Istanbul, finding a seat beside an Asian woman who seemed to be trying to crumple herself into the corner. "What do you do?" I asked at some intimately groggy part of the trip. "I'm a nurse," the woman replied as the bus continued down the flat highway, a drive only punctuated by one rest stop at a sprawl of buildings in the middle of nowhere containing a hive of '80s Atari games, pastry vendors and hole in the ground toilets, rows of them, the sinks hung with signs banning foot washing. "Why are you here?" I tried next and the woman had let out a primordial sigh, "Vanishing. Done with it all. On the road what five, six weeks. You?" I didn't really know the answer to that question or, more to the point, I knew but had little interest in telling anyone else. "I'm here to better understand my lover, to see where he came from. I'm here because I cannot have him and so I need his land instead." Yes, this was the real reason I had travelled to Turkey nine days ago. But what I tell the likely indifferent nurse is, "O adventure, why else?" smiling transparently as I do so, just another superficial lone female tourist aren't I, not this lunatic of love.

Strangely, with all the choices for travellers in this district, the nurse ends up a guest in the same B & B as me, a rundown cement block on the dusty outskirts of the district known deceptively as Sweet Tulip Hostel. Each room is fitted with only a bed and a dresser, the seamed walls decorated haphazardly with torn posters of fairy chimneys and other romanticized icons of the region. The toilets and showers are outside, thinly partitioned and cold. The first morning, I spot the nurse in the breakfast room, a space lined with benches on the roof of the B & B where guests consume hardboiled eggs, Greek yoghurt and clots of chocolate to the background noise of Turkish soap operas. She is sitting by herself, slowly sipping her Nescafé. Passing her, I manage a grin, "Going on the tour today?" But the nurse only glances up like a very old animal, "Not sure," before dropping her head back down to the Vincent Lam novel she is reading, or at least pretending to; I never see her turn a page.

Going on a tour. This is the one sane thing I feel sure I have accomplished so far on this sojourn, finally set up a logical little series of day trips for myself out in the country. The cost is somewhat painful but balanced out by the thought that, at last, I am coming to my senses, not straying about anymore, but finding an itinerary and sticking to it. The tour is going to show me a whole array of those fabled fairy chimneys, a ceramics factory, some underground houses, churches, roadside shrines, cemeteries. Stuff like that. A sensible tourist's ambitions. What I plan to see will have minimal relation to my lover's experience of growing up in the downtown core of Istanbul. I will drive him out of my mind in such fashion, play *flâneur* rather than archaeologist.

And, for two whole days, I have done just that. Watched Hasid spin a pot with his bare hairy hands, drank cups of ubiquitous apple tea at the rug manufacturers, gazed in a kind of moved disbelief at those towering rock outcroppings their guide, Evet, had described as fingers entwined, two camels kissing, a giant face in the desert. The third day though, I wake without a schedule and decide to go to the hammam. Which is where I see the nurse once more.

The attendant leads me to the showers, hands me wooden flip-flops and a plush white towel and leaves me to undertake my ablutions, followed if I so desire, by a sauna prior to the scrub and purification treatment I have paid for. The brochure shows pictures of naked women, their nipples topped by meringues of suds, reclining like goddesses on stone beds, but I am determined to keep my swimsuit on, a simple sleek one piece I only use once a year on a visit to my sister's place in Tofino. I'm relieved to see I'm not the only prude. Of the three women already in the sauna, one is wearing a tank top and shorts, another sports a puffy silver jumpsuit. She looks like the Pilsbury Space Girl, I laugh to myself, presuming the garb must promote weight loss. Indeed, the woman clambers out of the sauna several times while I am sitting on the bench, weighs herself after unzipping the spacesuit to reveal a plump olive body bound at breast and groin with wide bandeaus of cloth and grimacing, shaking her head, opens the door once more to the steam.

She doesn't speak English either and the only one who does, the third woman, the nurse, is slumped in the corner of the sauna, a white towel swathed around her as if she is broken. Her eyes closed, hands hanging by her sides, even her legs fallen open. Keeping them together must be too much work. I want to shake her now, yell, "Wake up! Why are you here, did you come to another country to die?" Perhaps an extreme reaction but the nurse's tremendous lassitude is beginning to unnerve me, even feel like a burden. If it was she who had been held captive and not me, would she have been able to summon the strength to resist, break free? Just how deep did this exhausted yielding go?

I open the door from the sauna, leaving the nurse behind me, and enter the hot room, a vaulted realm of raised beds with what looks like a giant sundial in the centre. A scarved woman gestures that I should lie down, slip off my suit. O god, why had I been raised to value privacy and concealment so highly? At swimming lessons throughout the '70s, my mother shepherding me and my three siblings into separate change rooms, her clucking noises over those women who paraded nude into the showers, shampoo bottles held aloft like torches. "No shame," she would tut, "no shame," as if feeling appalled by one's naked flesh was a cardinal virtue.

What the hell, who knows me here, I finally decide, yanking the straps down and letting the moist suit ball, drop to the tiled floor. The woman stands above my prone body with a cheesecloth, loads it with suds and begins to squeeze. Clouds collapse onto the plains of my flesh and then the kerchieffed lady starts to rub, laughing as she does so. At what? My obvious struggle to let go, relax? Over the pillules of dead skin that are now sloughing off me, curds, tumbleweeds? Death. Sloughing off me. A sudden jubilance. I raise my arms, let my mouth hang open. All that muscular tension falling away. "*Cok guezel*," the woman keeps uttering as she chafes the cloth upon me, and I know at least what this means, from my guidebook to basic Turkish phrases. It means "very beautiful." If it was only my lover saying such things, but no, I would never trust him like this, trust him the way I can a total stranger I am paying to scrub me down, wash me up, release me lighter into the world.

Things You Don't Want to Hear About, Johnny

I like Q-tipping my ears while taking a dump. It's better than sex, actually. Especially since I had that voluntary clitoridectomy because post-amputation it's too difficult to masturbate anymore and thus fucking became simple again, as it was when I was thirteen and flat and only a hole that boys wanted to stick things inside, a hole with long legs and badly permed hair. You probably don't want to hear this, Johnny, but once I took a piss in the middle of Broadway after drinking a supersized Bud Light super fast and after this I went to a park where I jumped on a complete stranger and asked him to do me. He was noble though and didn't and since then I've been trying to find him in every man but they all fail the test. One of them even had to drug me to prove I didn't really want to sleep with him because it made me purer that way and I woke with a taste of old oranges in my mouth and him handing me my panties like a poorly-written letter. You probably don't want to hear this either but I really like giving head. How it's soft and then hard and then soft again and I have the seed on my tongue and in my throat like I'm the earth and can grow the most amazing flowers of nothingness. But my pussy has stretch marks on it now from giving birth to all those elephants and flamingoes and serial killers, there is a moustache above one lip and a goatee below the other, sometimes I even wear a diaper and a bib, just for kicks, and I only feel sexy in my dreams anymore where (you definitely won't want to hear this, Johnny) I screw boys skinny as ropes of liquorice with skin like peaches and we fart and drool and all mount each other in the fading light like lost dogs of lust, so disgusting, Johnny, and perfect.

The Unspoken Sorrow of the Blarney Stone Man

All day long, he holds the brief bodies of strangers. They line up, in the harsh sun or spackling rain, thousands of them: Americans, Germans, a few Japanese, the youngest around eight and squirmy as cotton fish in his grip, the oldest perhaps in their seventies, arriving between his palms in stages of pained descent. When it's their turn, after they've spent up to several hours winding the 127 tightly-cut stone steps to the mythical spot where eloquence will be gifted them if they lie on their backs and arch their lips low in an upside-down smooch on that smooth piece of rock lodged in a centuries-old parapet, he tells them, "Grab on." To the two iron handles he means, the ones designed to poise them over the slit where they will lie, suspended, bereft of glasses, jackets cast aside, pockets emptied. His main job then is to place one capacious hand on either side of their waists: soft, bony, silken, belted, and say, "Lean back. Now kiss." And at that instant, the photographer to their left snaps a quick shot of their awkward benediction which they will later be urged to purchase at the gift shop in the Keep for only ten euros, including a certificate recording their triumph, apparently one of the ninety-nine things to cross off your bucket list before you die. The Blarney Stone man has no such list. He goes home alone and soaks his aching wrists in a bowl of Epsom salts. In his dreams, he necks with the Pillsbury Dough Boy and wakes on a wet pillow, though from drool or tears he cannot tell.

Dollface

Time had passed. I hadn't realized. No one had told me. Instead they still wanted me to model for them, wearing pinafores, sporting pin curls. Just yesterday I was hired to do a shoot where I put on a baby doll dress and painted my face brown as if I had just been playing in the mud. Making mud cakes, making brown, inedible cookies. The photographer was very short as he always is, like Tom Thumb or Tinkerbell. Even though he wears a top hat, you know he is short, so tiny he can't even see through the lens so his blind assistant has to check my poses, press the button down. While I was being Dollface with ribbons and a lollipop and the mud was fun, I drifted off and had a dream. In the dream, my body was long and stringy as if all the stuffing had come out. Also, there were spots on it. They were light red and dark red like rosebuds and rubber balls, only these spots hurt. And a man's voice kept yelling at me, "Just throw me in the dirt when you're done. That's where you should throw me."

No one noticed I was asleep, neither the small photographer nor his blind assistant. I had kept doing as I was told the whole time and so no one had known I was actually dreaming.

They told me, you're a dirty girl, a cute one, a real poppet, a sausage with frills on and what would momma say, her baby so muddy like that. That was the fun of it. That I was so very young and bad. At midnight, the shoot wrapped up and I took the bus back to Dollshouse. The tiny photographer and his blind assistant went for lattes instead. I kept my party frock on but washed my face a bit so it didn't look like I'd been playing in the mud, even for money.

On the bus, I spied a boy looking at me. He was five years old or fifteen. My age anyway, I thought. Somehow I had lost track. He carried a bag of cotton candy. Pink and blue puffs of it, fluffy, furry clumps of it. I knew he would want to share some of it with a Dollface like me and besides, he was beautiful, smooth as plums, shiny as tinsel. I reached out for some, smiling with my best dimples, curtseying with my adorably chubby legs, but all he did was scowl at me! He stared as if I wasn't Dollface at all but some yucky thing he didn't want to touch, something he usually only saw from a long way off and maybe threw rocks at.

"Get lost old lady," he spat, leaping off the bus with his bag of cotton candy swinging its dim and sugary lights further and further away from me. Then I caught sight of myself in the window. The night was so dark that I could see the mud hadn't left my face at all; it had settled into lines and creases and wrinkles my skin had suddenly thrown up, like I was ill forever now, the puke of being old lying everywhere you looked. Why was I Dollface then if I was only an old lady, smeared with the joke of mud puddle play, got up in a party dress from my youth.

That must have been in the last century now I think, when there were spinning tops and hoop skirts. No one had told me time passes. And here I'd been flirting with that boy, imagining his disgust was desire because after all I was Dollface and the short photographer and his blind assistant had wanted me. They had even given me Dollshouse where I eat off very small plates and the mirrors are as tiny as diamonds.

Shelf Life

Delia reads the ad over a poached egg after the kids leave for school.

Seeking still-beautiful women with scars & wrinkles for well-paid work. Flexible hours. Downtown Vancouver office. Please contact Mr. X.

At once, she is curious. Thirty-nine years old this May, she has indeed accumulated a variety of scars: innoculation punctures on her hip, a white reminder on her calf of a failed cartwheel attempt at eight, her first shave too had marred what could have been elegant gams, then there were the remnants of chickenpox, her three pregnancies' generous sprinkling of stretch marks and a C-section slash, grim, above her pubis. One cigarette burn; several knife marks born of her clumsiness in the kitchen; a dog bite. Yes, she is well-equipped to respond to this job ad.

Even more satisfyingly, her qualifications have lately been boosted by the continued addition of facial creases. It had started beneath the eyes, too easy to hide behind glasses, but now at last she possesses two hard etchings that cup her mouth, the early signs of a promising progression down to the neck and then the chest region: loosenesses, folds.

And yet she still sports a certain décolletage, long, impossibly thick hair.

Delia dresses as revealingly as the damp permits and flounces into the rather drab office. Would this be an advertising position? Do they need a model for a new line of cosmetics targeting the mature physique? Will she be required to test out unguents, pills, laser treatments? Most mysterious. What she'd begun to see as drawbacks in the ever-tightening job market must have become, at least here, assets.

Delia, broke, only hopes her scars, her wrinkles, are sufficient. Surely there will be other women vying for the opportunity who have endured mastectomies, hysterectomies, or who already look like O'Keeffe did in Taos. But perhaps there is more than just one position?

Delia is ushered into a brightly lit room, backdropped by a black curtain.

"Remove your clothes," a disembodied male voice speaks.

"All of them?"

"Why of course."

So she strips: her satin, her velour, dropping them on the floor like autumn.

The voice, which seems to be coming from a box in the corner of the ceiling, purrs.

"Good. Good. Turn. Turn please. Now bend over. Further. That's right. Nice episiotomy scar. Those always excite the gents."

Wonderful! She'd forgotten altogether about that one.

"So now I want you to pretend I'm a client. They will be watching you through that screen on the far wall. You won't see them. Just respond in the sexiest way you can to my demand and put all the hot actions you desire to them. Ready? Shall we begin?"

Delia stands under the bare lights, stroking the thin slit above her navel from that long ago exploratory surgery she'd had, what was it, a laproscopy. There is still the removal of her appendix to increase her earning potential in the short term. As for the long haul, the possibilities, she feels confident, are endless.

Alfie Flight, Welder & Bard

"In the tiny piece of colored glass my love was born"—Donovan

The Elders are wandering the streets again, or not wandering precisely I suppose as they are obviously on a mission. Elder Jim & Elder Bob are like all their kind, men never over twenty-one, hair shorn in angelic-army style, sporting dress shirts, slacks and ties, Bibles in hand, scanning avidly for wayward types to whom they can ask, in their gentle, insistent timbres: "Have YOU accepted Jesus Christ into your heart?" I think of the parodist on the Drive holding a sign reading "Our GRATE Lord, Cheesus Crust" but I respond, "Frankly, my heart has no room for another man," having just that morning taken Bradley between my thighs at least five times until we both lay slickered with jizz and panting out WOW. Although I've never actually said those words to Brad, I'm pretty sure he knows he's stuck quite securely between my ventricles, along with a few ghosts, some vagabonds, and my father, on his good days, perhaps. But my ticker has always been soft. Last week, for instance, I fell in love with a story a woman told me on a bus. Once a schoolteacher in Jacksonville, she used to have a student so talented a poet (she claimed) that "My dear, he regularly made me gasp with his iambics!" I asked her if she'd kept in touch with him over the years and she tossed her head like a morose pony, "For a time yes, but last I heard he was working the oil fields and not doing so well." Or maybe it was his name I fell for come to think of it—Alfie Flight—that fusion of yee haw and majesty. Either way, I'd been romancing him in my mind ever since, his innate musicality, his absolute lostness. There was still room for Bradley, without doubt, but not a smidge left for Christ.

Bite

The epitome of being human, Dahlia thinks, then and afterwards, is to act consciously in ways you will later regret. While, at the same time, rationalizing, as she has, that regret is not a word in her vocabulary, that it just might turn out otherwise, even given a vast array of contradictory evidence. Who, after all, can anticipate the range of factors in any given situation?

This has always been her problem. Sharing such a trait with so many other hapless humans in the universe is no real consolation. In fact, it makes things worse. She has not proven herself better, wiser, less susceptible to memory's sweet lies. She is only one of them, powerless against the haunting what ifs in the mind, willing to make a mess of everything good just to see if acting disastrously really will prove disastrous once again.

φ

Is it you?
Three little stinging words.

φ

At thirty-six, Dahlia is already on her third marriage. A certain restlessness, combined with the built-in temptations of her profession, the theatre, have made her seemingly incapable of staying with a man for longer than six years. Each relationship begins differently of course. Her first one started out of curiosity, an adolescent girl's ill-defined penchant for shacking up with any man who brings her roses and doesn't expect sex until at least the third date. She and

Vinnie had even procreated, a daughter named Lila, four-teen now, still living with him in the fixer-up house they had bought together off 6th Avenue and Victoria Drive. Barring an opening or a gala, Dahlia tries to visit Lila every other weekend.

The second man, Chas, was, still is, in the same profession as Dahlia. They met when she was playing Lucky to his Pozzo for the Driven Theatre Company. One of those cramped venues in the basement of a café. The run had been extended though and by the end of it she was relishing that whip, Chas's pomposity, the way he stormed around backstage, tossing black jellybeans into his mouth as if it was an entirely reckless gesture. She hooked up with him only a few weeks after she had left Vinnie. A relatively calm agreement. At the time she had been living in a grimy pad by the Broadway Skytrain and was all too ready to explore other options.

Lila had been nearly three when she split from Vinnie and Chas made it clear that he admired her maternal nonchalance, the dedication she showed to the vicissitudes of live theatre. When they ran short of cash, as frequently happened before their Fringe run began, Chas would do construction work for his father's company, Dahlia would waitress at Saucy Sue's, a breakfast joint on Main Street where all the menu items were named after Elvis tunes: Blue Suede Benny, Jailhouse Crepes.

For at least three years, she and Chas had been "Smokin' Hot," as their regular director, Bill Lahey, jazzed out whenever he saw them, shaking his hand about rapidly as though just the sight of them had set it on fire. Yet, without warning, only a few years in, Dahlia began to feel that distinct sense of becoming indistinct again, as if the relationship had ceased to have the power to define her, propel her in the world, the comfort of it turning her nebulous, wavering.

Affairs re-sharpened her psychic contours, tautened her physical sensibilities. After reading Sartre's biography, obviously none too closely, she and Chas had given open marriage a go, but becoming transparent, to the point of telling each other everything had, frankly, become exhausting. Further, such revelations, instead of increasing her sense of freedom, made her feel owned. Human beings feed on secrecy. That was the central joy in masturbating, Dahlia thought, one needn't tell anyone, the essential solitude of the act intensifying the pleasure, indeed lending it a kind of meaning.

Telling Chas all about her dalliances with Jay the lighting guy, Lacey, the girl who worked at Booster Juice and Miguel, the devastatingly seductive shoeshine kid, had only puffed Chas up to patriarchal immensities, enabling him to gorge on the once enticing sadism of his nature until he was more a grim confessor to Dahlia than a collaborative partner.

And then she had met David.

φ

Do you remember how we were, you my first girl, my first love?

She'd known he was her first, but not that it had been a reciprocal loss of innocence.

Was this what had clinched it?

She had to see him again.

φ

She had met David at Home Hardware. Dahlia had been buying a hummingbird feeder; he another set of wrenches. David, like Vinnie, worked at a more stable trade than theatre. Plumbing. Vinnie had been his uncle's lackey though, while David owned his own small outfit—"I Plumb Forgot." Vinnie had once tried to understand Dahlia's weird world, quizzing her about mnemonics and blocking over tea after they'd put Lila to bed. David, however, scoffed at her profession, in a lovingly jokey way—"Hey you aren't gonna call Shakespeare when you need your biffy unplugged are you then?" With his benevolent ignorance, he bequeathed Dahlia realms of silence and privacy to practise her art in.

She owes him for that, at least. Is determined this time to work things out, if only for the sake that, in her nearly late thirties, she is beginning to lose interest in starting all over again, recounting her weary and lengthening tale of failures and bit parts to new men. David is like a pot roast, a cosy blanket, uncomplicated, swaddling. Then that email had to arrive, out of nowhere, from that two decades dead ghost.

φ

Dahlia had scarcely known him, in the way that children take up friendships in elementary school based on the palest of resemblances and teenagers lock themselves into high school obsessions concocted from little more than the sight of a compelling forearm, a congruent scent. He had been tragic, an orphan. To her adolescent romanticism, that was sufficient. When he asked her to have sex with him in the last semester of grade nine, a query couched in the cursive desperation of notes passed to her during English class, "Please let's do it, no one will find out so why not?" she felt she had no choice but to acquiesce.

That day, they met behind the school and he hadn't said a word to her until they had walked down the street to the basement suite where he lived with his foster parents. "Take off your clothes," he told her with what she imagined was honed authority and she had stripped out of her blouse, her skirt, lay goose pimpled on the single bed, her body a band of light. As he entered her and she became juicy and aching, she had gazed up at his beautiful unknowability, grieving for losses she couldn't fathom, she with her wholesome mother, her suburban home, adopted him with her cunt like a saint, pledging to herself silently, "With this I will heal you" (she might even have thought "thee" as it sounded more fitting for the near-religious transformation he wrought in her).

And so began two years of fucking, mostly half-naked encounters that ranged across the majority of Greater Vancouver's parks, public washrooms, school gyms and laundromats. His favourite ploy though was to pursue her to the bus stop in front of Angel's Packers, snatch her transfer away like some urban Pan and hold it hostage until she'd sucked him off.

He seemed to derive the most pleasure from this tiny act of vengeance and lust, stroking her hair with a sweeping hand, saying he loved her as she opened her mouth over and over again to his frighteningly tumescent cock. After he came however, he would retract everything he'd said to her, tossing the transfer back as he tucked himself into his jeans, laughing, "Just said I loved you then. You know that's not true, right?"

Interpreting the grace in this, the balm, was difficult for Dahlia, but a challenge she took upon herself readily until the day when he and his foster family had moved to Fernie. They were sixteen. She had lost sight of him for twenty years.

ϕ

And now there it lies in her in-box: the banana in the split, the slug in the peonies. It's true she had asked for this, a raw memento of adolescence, but now what is she going to do with it? Kids Lila's age or maybe a little older would call it a Cock Shot. Apparently there was a whole section in the personals on Craigslist that featured men showing off their genitalia in the hopes that women would what, melt at the sight of the length of their members, go crazy for their weighty sacs?

Though she wanted to see him again, she was aware they had vastly differing agendas. He apparently wanted a reprise of their teenage summer of lust in a string of motels from Victoria to Vernon; Dahlia mostly just wanted to dine with him (or so she said), reminisce, though the notion, the more she considered it, was absurd. They'd never spoken, except with fingers, lips, here and there a few well-placed clichés: "You're the only girl for me," "I'll love you forever," platitudes plainly filched from episodes of *The Young and the Restless*.

So how would they begin now—with psychoanalysis, with nostalgia? With the banality of small talk after their extremes of arousal? He had asked her first for naked pictures: of her ass, which he recalled being "small as a handful," of her tits "they must have gotten bigger by now, eh?" and even of her cunt, the fantasied hairless past of it anyway, when it was his clenched passage to wedge into, split.

Though Dahlia had initially demurred, she had then compromised, sending him a bra and panties photo, before turning the tables (she had thought) by asking for a nudie pic in return, "for old times sake." If it was going to become a game again, she refused to be the only one laying her cards down, the only one reduced to her flesh though she knows now, even with such stakes, it wasn't equal, never would be. She would always be revealing more than him.

Nonetheless, she is surprised when he finally sends it to her. Had she imagined that her request would silence him, send him scurrying back, hands clutching his jewels, to his undoubtedly long-suffering wife? But he had scarcely flinched at her request, Dahlia thinks, staring at the image now before her: his shaft even thicker than she remembers, a wide flank half-hard, laid out against the canvas of his white tee, dark pubes flecking his heavy balls. He has snapped it with his cell. Probably at work. In his private office where he likely screws secretaries, the wives of associates. He never had any sense of shame, did he? His cock was only a tool, more impressive than a sports car, a yacht, because permanently his, used so many times by now, she imagines, that there is no vulnerability left in it, no aura of tenderness.

Though bewildered by the sight of it, Dahlia can't seem to delete the photo. Every morning, scrolling down to it, she feels the same desire, the same nausea. It is becoming a kind of therapy for her as she returns, over and over again, to the moment he first stuck it in her mouth. She could barely breathe. She felt suffused with a sense of reverence. What the hell was going on?

φ

They arranged to meet at Languor, a new canape and pastry joint that had opened up at the corner of Main and 25th. Neither of them mentioned its proximity to the bus stop that marked a primary site of their dalliances.

David never asked questions. A good thing in Dahlia's mind, but one that also inspired guilt. "If I gotta ask, it means I don't trust you baby," David would say, cracking another beer and settling down to watch the game. But did he recall so little of her past (she had disgorged all the major details on their first date: a BBQ at Stanley Park where he had insisted on cooking the steaks). An actress, a negligent mother, a repeat offender between the sheets, she was obviously up to no good. Maybe he doesn't care, she convinces herself. Perhaps as long as she is happy that is enough for David. Is she happy?

Full of anticipation, nerves, odd hopes. Not proud of herself for setting this up though. No.

It would have been so much cleaner had she written to this first love, this stranger:

"Thanks for looking me up. Good to hear things are going well for you (married nine years, he'd told her in an email last week when she'd pressed for more details, no kids, owns a bricklaying business in the Kootenays). I wish you the best."

And that would have been that.

But, along with telling her she had been his first lover, he had also revealed that, a few years ago, he'd nearly OD'd on junk, that the great passion of his twenties had committed suicide, pregnant with their baby. On top of all this, he had even apologized for the cruel way he had used her body, promised her an orgasm this time. If she would just give him another chance. Please baby, let me make it up to you! She hadn't agreed to this part though, said they would only meet on a platonic basis, that seeing him would be an act of closure, personal growth, moving on.

Language. How generous its lexicon of self-deception.

φ

What could be more terrible, more reassuring than the resumption of patterns?

Dahlia considers this as she takes his cock into her mouth, cold in the alleyway, twenty years older.

Hole

Seeing Johnny bleed was about the hottest thing Megan had ever watched. The gang in the living room playing Rock Band till 4 am, noodling for bright plastic fame—"Hella hella hella. Fuck!" all juiced up on Jager and popsicles and he suddenly wanting another hole.

The girl knew how to do it. She did. Had the gloves, antiseptic, measuring stick, Vaseline, needles. Professional-like. Rigged up a spot on the kitchen table, sweeping off ketchup chips, dog kibbles, Johnny plonking himself on a chair in his skin-tights, stripping off shirt, socks, lizard in the light of all those steel tools. She popped a dot beneath his lip, its hard snarl, the strip of hair below that, sharp runway, he only fifteen, her daughter's age for Christ's sake, shit, and how she couldn't lift her eyes from the bright tip as it tapped his flesh, slid in—"Just a jab, good kid"—then the blood released its streams—"Damn damn"—the girl trying to stopper it with tissues, plug the wound, red over Johnny's chin, down his violent-white chest, one trickle making it to his navel, the early curls of pubes crisping up from his waistband and that brutal silk of belly. No one else was watching. She didn't move.

"Hit a vein. Sometimes it happens." The girl, marking for another hole, a breath to the left of the first—"True that." Johnny's lids dropped, lashes gating his pale face as the needle entered him again, Megan hoping for another mistake, she could watch him bleed all day, shudders puncturing her like love.

The Mouth

When she leaned over and kissed the wacky-inflatable-arms-waving man at the frat house Hallowe'en party, a portal opened in her mouth as it pressed its cidery wetness against his marshmallow-soft cheek that peeked out of its round of fabric like a particularly ripe cheese. The portal was dark as portals are and whirling through it in the shapes of the kind of chintzy meteorites you might see on early episodes of *The Twilight Zone* were the faces of the boy-men she had ever kissed in her time, going on twenty years now she figured, of smooching these creatures when still somewhat coherently drunk, at gatherings where her essential loneliness sat like an old cupcake in her. What shocked her though was that all the faces were the same in this sad, whapping portal. Whap whap whap, the pliable, unfinished features flew past her, their wonky teeth or nebbish glasses or whether they had black or blond head fuzz failing to distinguish each from each, the general impression being one of gumball-scented youth and utter, total pointlessness. She had never been spontaneous or unique after all (the portal faces were sneering at her) but some type of machine that plugged itself into these sleek empty sockets and received a charge from them that never held, not really. Perhaps it was the fact that the wacky inflatable man had flinched as she pressed the once-gift of her lips on him that had opened this horrible portal of despair in her. At any rate, she was lonelier now than she had been before, flailing about in the whoosh of her past, while the arms-waving man retreated to a nebulous plastic speck somewhere between the sticky beer pong table and the two glow-in-the-dark hula hoopers with their bellies blank-slating her eyes.

La Roi Dagobert

Daz, the god of beauty and Band-Aids, rolls a spliff on the table of the Crowne pub, pinching the weed out of a silver lip-shaped tin, his fingers a tough yellow, the nails sawn down, patched, his face too, one on the temple and another on his bristled chin. "Yes, indeed, I like to dress up," he tells the girl when she fingers his tie on the dance floor, too long for his skinny little corpse but what the hell, it's shiny, spattered with Cubist bouquets and it clashes perfectly with his blue striped shirt, plaid pants and gilded earrings. Later, after he smokes a grape-flavoured cigarillo and does a couple of lines with her in the men's washroom, he'll tell her she looks just like the "divas of my youth baby, just like Janis Joplin, beautiful, that's what you are, crazy," and she will climax with him, though it damn well won't be him she's thinking about as she rides to wetness on her hungry cunt, no, it'll be that kid she likes to tool around with, a boy with hair like Mozart's, blond curls, spike in his tongue, mouth doing that Billy Idol sneer all the time, now *he's* on the up and up, Daz laughs to himself, hemmed in by pitchers of half-drunk draft, Montreal next, then where, Tijuana? But Lemmy's slurring "Dirty Love" low over the PA for now and somewhere in the dark distances a train aches its whistle into the night, an animal dragging itself over ravaged lands.

Bobbles

The first day of grade two, Jez slides down the fire pole. In a skirt. Thea is so impressed that she offers Jez her last piece of Bubbalicious. Jez takes it and they are suddenly friends for all eternity and back, which sounds like a very long time.

Thea watches Jez do the monkey bars, tires and twisty slide all in one recess.

Jez is like a tornado in girl form, whirling towards the playground and laughing in the way Thea imagines a tornado might laugh, not like Santa Claus as many people think, but in big whoops followed by skinny shrieks.

Thea, herself, can't even dream of clambering around on the monkey bars without trembling. There are many stories in the paper about concussions and teeth falling to the ground and sometimes eyes getting poked out and Thea is having none of it.

She likes to read at break instead while Tornado Girl whoops and crushes.

Lately it has been Pearl S. Buck's *The Good Earth*, leading her to add the word "concubine" to her vocabulary, though she still isn't sure how she can use it in a sentence.

φ

Jez and Thea are opposites.

But that's ok, Thea's mother tells her.

"Opposites attract."

"Why?"

"Well, you have things going for you Jez doesn't and vice versa. I mean look at Dad and me."

Thea looks. It's true that her mother likes making messes and her father likes cleaning them up, that her mother likes cooking borscht and that her father only wants to eat it.

So it could work then. Thea is pretty sure her parents have been married to eternity and back.

But Thea's mother and Jez's mother are also very different and that doesn't mean they are good friends. They'll do mom talk in the doorway though when Thea's mother drops her off at Jez's.

Jez's mom is like a bird, Thea's mother always says later, and o those high heels, her feet will be deformed in no time and then there's that frosted lipstick and her hair stiff as Dolly Parton's. So unnatural, Thea's mom tsks and tsks.

Jez's mom sells Avon. Thea's mom is a nurse who eats bean sprouts.

Soon Thea is spending every other Saturday at Jez's after her mom picks Jez up from her ballet and jazz dance classes.

At Jez's, Thea eats lunches of KD with mini dills and cocktail sausages. Dessert is white bread toasted with a whole field of sugar and cinnamon on top.

"Would you look at that kid eat," Jez's mom says to Jez's dad George. "She's like an African refugee for gosh sakes!"

And George sometimes ruffles Thea's hair even though it is cut with pinking shears.

Jez has French braids.

φ

Near the end of grade two, Thea finds out that Jez has a secret.

Everyone has a secret, Thea supposes, something you can't talk much about to most people, like if you have a concubine for instance.

Thea's secret is that she is a witch. Under her bed, she keeps a box with magical things in it: a golden chain, a purple handkerchief that transforms into different animals, a double acorn and such. When Thea really needs something, she makes a spell and it appears. She's even friends with Jez because of a spell she made. Maybe.

People think witches are bad and so that's why this is a secret.

Jez has a harder secret. It's harder because it is a person.

Once Thea sees Jez's secret she knows why Jez is Tornado Girl.

φ

Thea saw Jez's secret one Saturday morning, the first morning Thea had ever slept over.

They were watching *Bionic Woman* in the den. Jez has a whole room just for TV and games. It has cushions everywhere and curtains they are supposed to pull across the doorway when Jez's mother wants to sleep in.

"Watch whatever you want," she groans at them, "but don't bug me till after ten."

At home, Thea is only allowed to watch educational programming. At Jez's they watch *Knight Rider, Happy Days, The Six Million Dollar Man,* all the cartoons and their favourite, *Bionic Woman.*

Thea thinks that Jez will grow up to be the bionic lady with just a bit more training and bigger breasts. Jez practises by lifting the foam couch while she makes the robot squirrel kind of sound that they hear whenever the Bionic Woman does bionic things—"Dee dee dee dee dee."

Then the curtain opens. A woman is there, in between the two halves. She is on her knees like someone praying in the wrong place. She inches towards Jez and Thea. Thea thinks she is asking them if they want breakfast. Her voice sounds like she is gargling toothpaste.

"Did you fall off the monkey bars?" is all Thea asks.

The woman laughs then, softly, but she doesn't get off her knees.

She can't, Thea thinks, but no one will tell her why.

Jez just stands, clutching one of the cushions like a shield.

"Hi. I'm Jez's sister. Julie. Pleased to meet you," the woman on her knees gurgles again.

Thea knows she is supposed to shake hands when she meets strangers.

But there must be other rules for meeting strangers on their knees.

Jez has been standing still for so long she isn't even Jez anymore.

Then she grabs Thea's hand, "Let's walk Pepper."

"In our pyjamas?"

"Sure. Why not?"

φ

Thea's never been outside in her PJ's before. Hers are flannel with cows jumping over the moon on them. Jez's are silky pink ones with bows over the nipples. They don't even put shoes on. Jez wants to get out of the house that fast.

Thea doesn't much like Pepper. He bites toes. But he's ok on a leash. They walk down Jez's block and through the park on the corner.

Thea wants to ask about Julie, why she's on her knees, why she's old, why she hasn't ever seen her before now. There are no people who live on their knees in any of the books Thea's read. But Jez is walking too quickly and Thea's mouth doesn't make any of the sounds she wants.

At the other end of the park, there is a building with a cross on it and a man sitting on its steps. "Hey girls," he calls to them.

Pepper doesn't seem to like the man much but the girls walk over there anyway. Jez is always curious about things.

The man smells a bit like he's been making mud pies. Grownups must still do that sometimes, Thea thinks.

"Girls, can I ask you a favour?" the man says, making kissy noises at Pepper. Favours are things people want you to do that you'd never do without being asked, Thea remembers.

"What?" Jez asks, twirling Pepper's rope like she's going to play a skipping game. *Ketchup, mustard, vinegar, salt,* Thea chants in her head.

"Well, you see," the man tells them, "I got a bit of a collection going and I wonder if you'd help me add to it."

Jez is zipping up and down the stairs now, Pepper barking and barking. Thea thinks she looks like a silky bolt of pink lightning.

"What of?" Jez asks as she dashes past him.

"Socks."

"O!" Thea and Jez say together.

"Girl's socks especially. The kind your mother hasn't washed yet. You wouldn't happen to have any of those would you?" He looks down at their feet.

"I collect Tic Tac boxes," Thea says, trying to make the man feel better about his odd collection.

"Good, good... then you know what it's like... collecting things."

"We have bobble socks mostly," Jez says then, stopping on the bottom stair for a moment, "like these ones."

Thea watches as Jez's leg kicks up into the air, nearly hitting the man, a long swooping tree branch with a cap of cotton snow on the end of it.

"O, those will do nicely," the man looks closely at them like an expert. "They will be perfect in fact, girls."

Jez glances at Thea and then they both crouch down and strip off their socks. They are all stained with grass now but the red bobbly bits are still bright.

The man seems very grateful as he shoves them in his pocket and then they are both racing down the street, feeling the scrape of cement on their soles, running Pepper back home, knowing, in this eternity world, that there are all kinds of secrets.

Breeders

Jackson loves rabbits. Anything stray really. On their first date, he had driven Mins to the parking lot behind the Black Creek McDonald's. Midnight. Hour of romance. But when he leaned towards her across the front seat of his Buick, it wasn't to kiss her but to grab an old bag of buns from the glove compartment.

"They'll be here soon," he hushed as if gangsters were on their way with the ransom for that precious bread-crammed sack. Then he guided her hand into the plastic opening (at least here she felt lust's first little tingle), swung the doors wide, and snapped off the interior light. She watched him as he tore the white buns into chunks. She did the same. They both flung them over the asphalt like pieces of moon and waited. Within seconds, tiny dark cats had emerged from the crevices in the building, falling upon the stale bread like the Israelites when God commanded manna to descend from Heaven. Mins suddenly recalled this tale from catechism class, her question about the connection between manna and the Host that no one could answer.

Jackson was a benevolent saviour but not, for the most part, a humble one. Mins got the idea that he was flaunting his cat-feeding ritual in the way that other guys would brag about their collection of video games or their buffed-up Mustangs. When the bag was finally empty, Jackson had leaned back, arms behind his head. He glanced at Mins, surveyed his herd of feline supplicants in their ravenous mewlings over his scraps and sighed, "Loveliest babies, aren't they doll?"

She'd never heard a boy say lovely before, never mind doll. They were seventeen for god's sake.

φ

Jackson loves his rabbits most though. They aren't allowed cats or dogs in their apartment complex. The landlord makes that clear. Right off the bat. He doesn't even want to rent to them with a kid. "Better not hear a peep outta that guy" he warns them the day they move in, Mins carting their minor possessions into the three-storey walk-up on one hip, Steven on the other, eighteen months old, still sucking on his baba.

The landlord sports very old tattoos on his forearms, a disintegrating Betty Boop, eroding anchors. "Lots o people work the night shift here. Don't want no complaints or I'll hafta get him a muzzle." Mins knows this isn't a joke. He even holds both furred hands up, miming a choking motion.

They probably aren't allowed rabbits either, but it isn't in the agreement they have signed in his apartment, just down the hall from theirs. Jackson and Mins have now been an item for twenty-eight months. A few weeks after they had fed the cats for the first time, they had taken each other's virginity on the floor of his parents' basement, a moist episode of fumbling that had given her rug burn and gotten her pregnant.

"Such is the beneficence of the universe," Jackson had intoned, "It's fate, Mins," upping his hours at the warehouse so they could move out together. Until this glorious, long-awaited day of relocation they had been living in the same basement Stevie had been conceived in. A brown Naugahyde bar from the '70s in one corner. A sink that backed up with her in-laws' garburator until a plume of waste shot up out of the drain ("Land ho!" Jackson would laugh).

Worse, the bocce ball alley that Jackson's father Santos had set up in the garage for himself and his Italian cronies. At least twice a week, they would be woken to the nicotined husks of cheers as balls banged and cracked into other balls, smoke purling beneath the door, no matter how much Mins tried to plug it with towels.

Finally, they had their own pad.

But Mins can't help saying, "I don't feel so welcome here, Jackson."

"Because of Mr. Peller?" he replies while putting their few pots and pans away. "O don't fret my lassie. He's nothing but a blowhard."

Mins suspects that Jackson read that word—blowhard—in *Moby Dick*. Jackson has been thumbing through it on his weekends off from the warehouse, often while they sit on the bench at Central Park feeding the ducks.

"No bread for these fine gentlemen though, Stevie," Jackson directs at his son as they fling smatterings of grain towards the lily-clogged pond. "Bread only engorges those duck tummies. Before long—poof, boom—implosion!"

Sometimes Jackson talks like he comes from another century that never even happened, Mins thinks.

φ

Jackson loves rabbits to excess. Behind the warehouse on Production Way, where Jackson works shelving end units, barbeques, wading pools and bulk flats of noodles, there is a field. Half a block's worth of scrubby grass, a weeping willow. People toss things there: boxes, condoms, tires. They also ditch their unwanted bunnies. Especially after Easter.

"Hah, out of the basket, they aren't so dashing anymore, are they? What did they think they were getting Master Junior, some plush insensate thing? O ye gods, I should take the cudgels to them!"

Jackson rants on in such a manner to Mins every night when he comes home from his shift to one of her three menu options: mushroom soup, sausages in buns and veggie stir-fry with baby shrimp. He barely pays attention to Steven apart from the mini-lectures he wags at him on the essential nature of personal responsibility and the undeniable evidence for the animal soul.

"Really Jacky," Mins has to object at times, "that's way over his head! We spent the day building Duplo and watching Barney. Talk how kids like, will you?"

Jackson begins staying late at work to feed the rabbits. He takes out all the carrots from the bags of chopped veggies Mins buys and even some of the celery too.

"You should be my witness," he gasps out when he finally returns while microwaving his dinner, or as he claps Stevie's splodgy hands together, "O so many bunnies all munching their repasts, just like Peter Rabbit."

Finally Mins has found a way for Jackson to spend time with his son. She picks up rabbit stories for him to read to Stevie before bed. *Benjamin Bunny. Mr. Rabbit and the Lovely Present. The Flopsy Bunnies.* Bugs Bunny. Sometimes Mins wonders when this will all end.

φ

Jackson's love for rabbits has become his defining characteristic. He starts calling Mins Bunnykins and Wabbity. When they have sex, he only wants to mount her from behind and pump her. Very fast. He has taught Stevie to do a bunny face where he squishes up his nose and snuffles. They now have many videos of this feat.

The first rabbit he brings home from the field he calls Rufous. Rufous is followed in rapid succession by Blinks, Hoppy, Madame Tutu, Ahab (he is still reading *Moby Dick*), Queequeg (ditto), and Domino. Jackson builds a set of hutches along one wall in their living room.

When Mr. Peller comes knocking though, it is Mins who has to answer the door and tell lies. "Um, he's just building a playpen to keep Stevie in, keep him quiet. Um. Like you want."

She is terrible with authority figures. Becomes butter. Becomes mush. But Mr. Peller seems placated, yells down the hallway, "Better be a damn big cage for that kid you're making, Jackson!"

The rabbits snort and wiffle loudly in their hutches. Straw flies through the wire and sticks in the shag carpet. They gnaw on carrots and alfalfa all day long. Sometimes they claw through the wood and lope around the living room while Mins is having her nap, chewing through telephone cords, baby toys, leaving little black pellets behind them like crumbs to show them where the path home is.

Jackson now rushes back after his shifts to spend the evening with them. Mins is starting to get worried about Stevie, how he stares at the hutches for hours, nose twitching, his eyes as empty as if he were watching endless reruns.

φ

Jackson loves his rabbits so much he forgets that they die.

On the morning that he is surprised by Hoppy's death, Mins realizes that, until now, Jackson has never had any pets at home and thus no experience of their inevitable demises. Rabbits and ducks and cats have, until that moment, been eternally replicating bodies of hunger and adorableness for Jackson. They are but endless founts of neediness, immortal embodiments of gratitude.

The dawn that Hoppy passes on, Jackson is getting ready for his shift and Mins is sitting in bed doing an Easter bunny puzzle with Steven.

"O my sainted aunts, no!" she hears Jackson wail. Now where did he get this expression from? Mins wonders whether Jackson is conscious of such borrowings, how odd they can be when set against his burliness, his bass voice. His love for rabbits another example of the awkward collisions in his character.

He is standing in their bedroom with Hoppy, the placid grey rabbit, cradled in his arms, right below his warehouse nametag. The rabbit is spasming; its bud of a mouth froths.

"We must fetch the vet, Mins!" Jackson is hysterical.

"O Jacky, vets can't help bunnies. And we don't have the money anyway. You know that." Why must she always be the voice of reason?

"But we can't just let the poor dear suffer!"

"It'll be over for her soon. Look she's already going stiff."

Stevie looks too, one of the puzzle bunny's ears clutched tightly in his fist.

Jackson seems flushed. "When the rabbit dies. You know what that means, Mins. Don't you?"

"No." What now?

"It means you're preggers. About to undergo a confinement. It's a sign. Are you prego, Mins?"

Well, her breasts had been more than a bit sore for the past few weeks now. But she wasn't regular most months. Hard to tell really.

"Guess I should get a check-up. Make sure."

"O yes. Yes you should at that. The rabbit knows my snookums. Hoppy knows."

Mins suddenly thinks of all the other bunnies in their living room hutch. They would also die. And would it always mean the same thing?

His vision of live children springing relentlessly from the corpses of dead rabbits, Hoppy living on in Julie or

Matthew or whoever else she might give birth to. Mins isn't sure what she's gotten herself into.

Jackson is swaying in the doorway now, crooning some kind of hymn to the dying rabbit as the bunny's hind legs punt out rigidly into paradise.

The Resurrection

The crazy thing about being a freelancer, Cass often thinks, is that while one is writing about the world, becoming an instant expert on everything from shiatsu to the stock market, the real world tends to disappear.

The more deadlines Cass sets for herself, the less she leaves her house. Five days it's been, of sloppy dressing gowns and Mr. Noodles, when Cass hears about her grandfather's death.

Her mother calls from Vancouver to tell her. December and it's raining there. Her mother isn't crying but she is raving on in the way Cass has noticed people in grief often do, all their memories of the deceased flickering before their eyes and spilling from their mouths in random compilations.

"We used to ride our bicycles through Sabden... o a long way, miles... went with him to deliver the host too... old Elsie depended on him, she did... he's a right proper gentleman, she'd say... all that time spent at his allotment... gooseberries he grew, big as your head, radishes... made tea on that hotplate... and did he love to dance, the foxtrot especially, though mother never liked it much... do you remember how he cried when the princess was killed?"

Cass wonders which stage of grieving this is according to Elizabeth Kubler Ross. Probably the second or first. Cass's mind tends to wander when she's on the phone as she tries to multitask around the lump of the receiver. She is trimming the rosemary plant now; then she is scrubbing the windowsill.

"Yes, Mum," she manages and she does, it's true.

An odd thing to recall of the man, perhaps. The last time she'd seen him, in the den of his Manchester brownstone, right after news had come of the car accident in the tunnel, the blood on Di's pricy white pantsuit.

How he'd wept, stumbling against the furniture as if his life had just become an obstacle course he couldn't fathom. What was really memorable though was how he'd used an old sock to staunch those tears. A grey one that had gradually become black with dampness. She knew he had handkerchiefs. Her grandma even ironed them. Had this sentimental gallivant into weeping called for something so out of the ordinary?

There is no love lost between Cass and the royal family. Not even the naughty side.

She consoled herself at the time that this highly publicized, essentially crass death had merely served as a trigger, one enabling her grandfather to cry about the friends he'd lost in the war perhaps, before he'd been sent to an Italian prison camp where he'd dragged out the remainder of the combat eating oatmeal with flies in it.

That day she'd gone back to Canada. Ten years ago. He had grown even older. And now he is dead.

"The worst thing about it, Cass, do you know?"

"No, Mum."

She tries to still her mind. Focus on her mother's voice, the pain that's creeping through the gaps between them.

"Your uncle Will says that the doctor told him the heart attack was so terrible that it tore his poor heart in two. It did. Right in two. Poor poor father. Too much love in it. Couldn't hold it without bursting, could it?"

Yet another example of the raving Cass is talking about. Instead of drawing her closer to her mother's suffering, such outbursts just make her feel pity for her weakness.

Fool of loss. Incapable of just seeing death for what it is, biological, cruel.

When Cass was twenty, her best friend's father had succumbed, much too young, to liver cancer. She had gone to visit him one day in palliative care (they had been close, he was a reporter, he read Chaucer) to find his wife bridged over his corpse, weeping and laughing hysterically.

"O Cass, I tell you," she'd whipped a glance at her, red and dark and moist, "just take a look at this. Look at his smile! Was he not a happy man passing out of this world. Proof in the pudding of the afterlife, baby!"

And so she had looked. And seen only a mouth wrenched up on one side in a final spasm of agony. And lost a kind of faith. Not in any possibility of heaven, that had left her at around six, but in people themselves. How delusional they all are.

She hung up on her mother after having promised to write a kind of eulogy for her grandfather, an in memoriam from the Canadian contingent. Being a writer, this is her lot. Only it is hard, she finds, to research oneself into feeling.

Cass is suddenly desperate to get out of the apartment. She doesn't drive, can't own a car anyway on her freelancer's budget, but, living in downtown Edmonton, she doesn't have far to walk to get to what she needs.

It's damn cold though. She knows that much about the world, the Google homepage updating her on a daily basis. Around minus twenty now. 5:36 pm. Cass pulls on long johns, cords, a sweater and a toque. Her favourite leather trenchcoat. The scarf with the candy canes on it her grandmother sent her last Christmas. Mittens. Boots.

Maybe she'll get a coffee at Ariba's, sit in Churchill Square for a while. What a hermit she's become. "You'll never get married at this rate," she hears her mother snapping.

As she walks down 100th Street, past expensive steak houses, the library, the CBC headquarters, Cass is startled to see the lights. Jesus, she'd completely forgotten about this annual ceremony.

The mayor is there, literally hundreds of foreign exchange students, cameras slung inside muffs, moms with toddlers tottering stiffly about in their snow suits, teenagers attempting to slide down the frozen railings.

The lights have just been lit, purple and blue ones on the twenty-foot tree with its teetering star, red ones on the Santa, candy canes and reindeer that cluster all over the last patch of grass in the square, now hidden under several feet of white.

Cass wants to turn around and dash back to her apartment, to her isolated petri dish of a life. But instead she just stands there, on the edge of it all, stamping up and down to keep the blood flowing, watching her breath become visible again.

Pollen

The woman across from me keeps buying flowers. She puts them on her patio. Flowers in pots, plastic, ceramic and the flowers are sun, lilac, cosmos, African violet. When I open my window, the crowd of smells rushes into my prim living room where the settee purses its comfortless lips, the colours sing too ebulliently from the corners of my eyes as I try to sip my tea, Carlos the cat punctuating my feet. Every day, the flowers. And each night, the voices. Just noises really. Loud of his, a burr through the walls. And her wailing, hard soft hard. I could ask myself why doesn't she leave him but I know something about how books become indistinguishable on the shelves and even limbs in the dark bed blur. She must rise before it's light to buy the flowers. Melody's Blooms. A short way down the street. Opens at 6 am. He leaves even earlier than this. She breathes breathes breathes awhile. And by the time I can see her through the slivers of my blinds she is bending over petals, placing yet another pot down on the cement, then turning to go back in.

Fruits

When she ran into him, after a year of absence, at that poetry reading at the Whoville deli, she knew instantly he was on the Cherry Hormone and perhaps aiming to advance to Orange Surgery. The gingham shirt he now wore poked out at the pleats and she was sure she could see the blunt ends of stems becoming fully erect when Patti Poetaster swooned her famed line, "Verily, like Heaven's glove, we fit." It was a little strange spotting him at the start of his Orchard phase but who was she to talk, having recently added to her Juiciness Factor by getting those Papayas implanted. Her motivation—not to compete with those Fruit Queens who graced so many covers of magazines in the Grove—no, but only to flesh out her flagging skin post the birth of all those Blackberry Babies who had suckled her Apples to Mush. Still, she was no longer allowed to judge what different kinds of fruit people needed to become—there was so much yearning towards perfection—like that woman across from her on the train heading to Harvest—pregnant belly huge enough she was likely to soon birth a Watermelon—yes, it's been known to happen—in the future they may all emerge that exquisitely pickable, that sweet.

Muses

Food I Ate with Frank

1. Fried kielbasa slathered with brie

Frank's mother never keeps such food in the fridge. You can tell by the way he hefts the sausage in two hands, like a little boy his first time up to bat, how he unwraps the cheese as if it is a silver-coated gift—"Space Truckin' " he jazzes out while rummaging for a knife to chop the whole thing up.

Alex, the acid man, is at the computer, scrolling down his list of MP3s.

"Danzig or Marianne Faithful, girl?"

"Don't you have any CDs, real ones?"

"What do you mean, girl, that's the past, this is the totally new wave. How come Alex knows this and he is just poor Russian immigrant?" he jokes, grating his r's into sharp flecks of sound.

"Ok, you pick then, Mr. Knarfusion."

Frank is slicing sausage like he's conducting Sibelius, mashing the snow of cheese on each chunk and tossing them over his shoulder into the splatting pan.

"Mother… tell your children not to walk my way, tell your children not to hear my words, what they mean, what they say, Mother."

His voice is low with a ghost of a lisp in it, but when Alex clicks the Danzig track, Frank sings rowdier, yelping the O in mother, air guitar shredding on the butcher's knife.

"Whoa guy, whoa, whoa," Alex jumps up from his swivel chair and snatches the knife from Frank, "maybe I better do the dinner thing, dude, what's she gonna think, trying to sleep, eh."

Alex's mother is always trying to sleep. She gets head-
aches. When she is awake though, sitting on the crumbed-
up couch, smoking and pale, she often laughs out loud, a
black seam plowing through her tired gold hair, and says,
"Always young and beautiful, us Russians, no Alexei?"

Frank's arms hang down and he has stopped singing.

The oil celebrates with little sparklers.

Alex tosses some napkins and an Easy Squeeze bottle of
ketchup on the table.

Turns to me, waving his precise hands—"Gogol would
approve... hey, you wanna show your titties to the web cam
before dinner?"

2. Pizza, two mediums with extra meat and a side of poutine

Frank takes me to meet his mother. She is working as a
live-in helper for a ninety-seven-year-old lady in Two
Mountains.

"At least she'll be dressed this way," he assures me,
striding over the train tracks that divide the industrial zone
from the 'burbs. He is wearing the same suit he always
wears lately, a navy blue number with shoulder pads and
a polka-dotted tie. The end of it is coated in dried Shish
Taouk sauce. Frank likes his suit.

"Eh qu'est qui arrive, les chums?" he says a lot when
he is wearing it, the cut of the pants making him swagger.

His mother is looking pretty sharp too. Her hair glazed
like an Easter ham and not even an apron over her cro-
cus-coloured dress though she must have been changing the
old lady's diapers all day or whatever helpers do.

"Where's the grub?" Frank barks out, pushing past her
and her two nippy terriers, busting through the glassed-in
swinging door.

Smells of grease, curdled things slither out.

"Francis, you get back in here right now and stop acting like all those bummy friends of yours! I tell you," she wags her finger at me, "he's just like his father."

Munching sounds come from the kitchen. Then the door sails back and Frank leans out, a pizza crust jabbed between his lips like a freshly cut cigar.

"Hey, you lookin' at me? Ah say, you lookin' at me?"

Maybe he thought he was The Godfather trying out for Taxi Driver.

It's always hard to say with Frank.

3. A sizeable pyramid of fortune cookies

Soupe et Nouilles on St. Catherine's is where we always eat when we visit Ken.

Ken is on methadone. "Makes me want noodles," he says so we pick him up Styrofoam coffins full with sometimes a clump of sweet 'n' sour pork on the side if he's moved enough weed that week.

Most of his customers are paras or quads, rehab buddies of Evan's, his roommate who'd been paralyzed in a bike accident right after grad. Ken has to turn him so he won't get bedsores and read him *Last Exit to Brooklyn* over and over again. On Fridays, his twin sister Lucy comes over and does lap dances for Evan, bobbing her new silicone breasts up and down—"Saved up for them, didn't I?" she tells us. "That's tricks, fellas."

"Wanna somma ma shtuff?" Ken, mouth crammed, gestures to the slithery mess in front of him. I glance at Evan's Husky dogs snuffling at the hoisin sauce. Hitler heils and heils on TV.

"That endless fucking history channel!" Evan calls out from the bed. "No wonder you're a goddamn junkie, Ken!"

"Was, man, dammit, was." Ken slapping Evan's stuck-there body with a noodle, brown drips flying to the wall and staying there.

Frank shakes the white baggie in his hand. "Got our own hits right here, my good sirs, little injections of the future."

There are at least twenty-eight cookies in there. I'd watched him reach behind the till and load up. Later on we lie on his mattress in St. Henri and he cracks each taupe shell open.

One swift snap and the slip of paper.

He doesn't even read them but there they are. All those possible outcomes in his lap, falling.

4. Cheap steaks with mushrooms and international flavours, hazelnut

Frank picks me up from Dorval at 3 pm.

"I did a bad thing," he says as we wait for my bag to spin towards us on the black carousel.

"What?"

His hair sticks up in the shape of the spaces between his fingers. He punches his arm out towards me, shoving his sleeve to the elbow.

"Jesus H."

My bag vanishes behind the rubber strips, too fast to grab. Frank's arm is swollen to the size a blood sausage, the skin greens and yellows around the lips of a recent puncture.

His pupils the diameters of the ends of sentences.

"We have to get you to the hospital. Now."

"Ok, ok, but swing me one of those Shastas first, will ya?"

Dollar pop in his other hand, Frank leads the way to the taxi station.

I suppose I'll be swinging this one too.

φ

Hours later, we are climbing the stairs to his three and a half.

I ditch my bag on his couch and dump the two loads from Safeway in the kitchen.

"Nice," I say to no one in particular, gazing around.

There is no toilet paper in the bathroom, no sheet on the bed and only a view of the back alley from his foot-wide balcony.

Frank has a bandage slathered around his arm.

"J'ai, ah, injecté le coke et c'etait infecté, je pense," he'd explained to the nurse in his butchered French.

On the way back, he had wanted groceries.

"I'll make dinner."

"You better," I say, watching him now with some anticipation, the coins of meat darkening in the pan surrounded by curves of mushrooms.

Frank brews instant coffee, glups in cream.

"Should try it. The best, man."

I'd spent five hours on the plane from Vancouver, three in the hospital and one in Safeway. I'm not about to pour my own coffee and Frank isn't going to take the hint.

Etiquette is, he often says, for the clones.

We play Hangman while dinner simmers, circles and lines dying all over the paper.

In the alley, gulls yelp, white bodies hunkering over a torn loaf.

"Ope, it's ready." Frank jumps up and with one arm slides the whole pan's worth onto one plate, pulls out a saucer for an ashtray and sits down again, poking his fork into the tough meat, gnawing a ring of fat off the steaming edge. He doesn't look over at me, my empty place, once.

I nearly cry then, so serviceable I am and invisible, too transparent for hunger.

5. Hot pot

We take the train to his father's from the station just below the psych ward.

"Don't talk about drugs or gangsters. Don't talk about my small penis," Frank cautions me as we knock at the apartment door.

His father's hair is thin. He has lots of golf trophies.

"Nobody makes hot pot like I do," he brags the instant he's whisked us into the plush environs of his condo on Nun's Island and introduced us to his "belle lady, Yvonne," a woman of bones and haute couture.

There is so much we can't speak of.

Frank's father chops, dices, slivers in the galley kitchen and we don't talk about his ex-wife, his twenty years in jail, his son's seventeenth admission to the psych ward.

No one asks about the record label Frank is trying to start or the movie he wants to shoot.

I am in town to give a reading at The Yellow Door, I venture, stories from a skinny volume called *Mainlining*.

"Stories, eh," Frank's father pipes out. "Used to read those myself, back a ways, liked those, what d'ya call them, detective books."

"O he did," Yvonne perks up, sleeking her skirt over her thighs and gleaming her brash teeth at us, "read them so fast, he did, like you wouldn't even believe."

"Can't sit still long enough anymore" he laughs. "Action's where it's at now, eh boy?"

Frank is fiddling with the magazines Yvonne has laid out, opening and slamming the front covers of *Chatelaine, Marie Claire, Scientific American.* "Yup."

A pot, spitting with oil, is being carried over our heads and placed on the overly long table.

"Now sit down, sit down will ya, and let me show you kids the ropes."

Ominously jovial, he instructs us in the art of spearing shrimp, dipping their coral curves in the vat, scooping gaudy hunks of peppers onto our plates, hefty rolls. Then over and over again, thrusting the shrimp into that hot little bath.

Frank sits at the far head of the table like a misplaced patriarch, sporting that suit and a shiny look in his eyes I want to think is the afterglow from the sex we'd had yesterday on his last hospital pass. An hour for twenty bucks in a hotel room on St. Laurent and most of that time he'd spent unlacing my twenty-hole Demonias, intent on pulling each lace out individually, his passion for the specificities, the boundaries, of process.

6. Rhubarb pie with Miracle Whip

Olga runs the reading series from the basement of a community centre in the McGill ghetto.

Each performer is introduced with the same flat Romanian irony. For a small donation, you can nibble on crackers, cookies, sip lukewarm Red Rose in a paper cup.

Frank shows up late.

I have just started to read my story, "Berube at Club Chaos," when he clomps down the stairs and crashes his way into the front row. Frank is wearing his duffle coat and a twill cap like Holden Caulfield. Olga glints disapprovingly at him over her glasses.

I finish my tale of a piano-playing punk and sit down beside him amid a light fall of applause. Frank leans over to me, whispers in my ear.

He can be cruel. I never know what he is going to say to me, what he will do.

"You're gorgeous" is what he says.

He can be very cruel. I am prepared for tragedy, I think, disaster, even common rudeness, but not this little perfect moment, this generous rupture.

Afterwards, we walk to Café Etranger. I feed him scarlet fruit pie with cream on top in a swirl white as martyrdom. "Vive le Frank libre!" he crows with his bad teeth, a glorying full of half-chewed dessert.

Love is a too-tight seed in my heart then and it will burst and grow a tree and he will chop it down.

7. Kraft dinner with a scoop of margarine on top

"You know when I knew I was white trash?"

We are crashed on the mattress in St. Henri, scabs of tobacco clinging to our skins.

I am staring at the yellow condom on the floor, his seed knotted inside it, a teaspoon of white.

"Michelle and I were cooking KD at her place."

"Michelle?"

"Went out with her in high school, my Michellelelelelelele," Frank whoops out.

"O."

"... and we were using a wooden spoon for the marg... hey that reminds me, when you were at Alex's last weekend, this girl picked me up in Le Biftek and she asked me to spoon... you know how fucked up I am I thought she meant drugs not... you know... so the marg was sliding down the noodles... you ever let a chick suck your tits, hippie Hesus?

I let a guy blow me once. It was ok. You're too straight aren't you, geek girl, nerdy wordy, hoe the row, you're one in a million, yeah, that's what you awawa, you're one in a million babe, you're a shooting stawawa."

Frank likes singing Guns N' Roses but will never do the Axel Rose dance, not even drunk on thirty Rickards, not even if I beg him to.

8. Perogies and onions in tomato sauce

Frank rode the Greyhound to Vancouver once, ten months before he died. Three-and-a-half days of sleeping in the aisles and eating fries with squishy packets of mayo.

The last time he'd tried to get to the Coast had been in a $400 Chevy Impala that had broken down on the 401.

He had had nothing to drink and so he lay down in the middle of the highway and waited to be run over. Now he has steel bars in his legs. They give him a pirate limp that would have gone good with the suit but it had been cut off him after the accident.

While I dump thawed perogies into a pan, toss strands of onions on top and douse the pale entanglements with a thick sauce, Frank yanks out his guitar and starts playing his latest song, "Hello Dear Friend, Dear Lover."

It isn't about me.

The song ends.

I hear a chair bashing against the wall as Frank lunges forward to kiss me, the head of his guitar hitting my shoulder, his new hospital-grown beard piercing my cheek.

"That song's not about you," he says, his kisses puncturing me, the perogies barely surfacing beneath their dark pond of sauce.

"I already knew that," I say.

9. Soup

Frank's best friend, Ricardo, has a mother called Maria. She likes to cook soup, he says, I shouldn't worry about it. There is snow everywhere in Two Mountains.

March 1st he had jumped.

At the funeral there are only inhospitable broccoli spears, throat-raking Triscuits.

Maria likes to make soup, says it will cure everything, even the sight of this: the doll-bodied Frank stuck into an old man's suit and my tears over him.

She serves it on a tray. It is perfect. Slow steam from the bowl. Sprigs of parsley. Delicate sheets of bread. Of course, I just look at it. And, at some point, it grows cold.

10. A bag of scones

"My father made them," Frank tells me. Nothing in his fridge but mustard, milk, rolls of film and a plastic bag of miniature scones, scrunched tight as socks.

He'll never eat them, I think.

This way, they stay a gift.

Muse

I, detrital.

This is how I will begin, I think.

My sweater is getting heavier.

I only want one glimpse of him, just a slip of a look, as he steps from his shininess, as he does every day of the week, and heads into Athena Taverna, the restaurant he owns on Iris Avenue where the smells of retsina and lamb live, the place the river whittles past but, well, I am not my own self anymore, the Idylls have me and my history is theirs.

The other day I thought I saw my daughter in the street. I yelled at her as she sat at the Italian Plaza,

"Don't you remember me, Therese? The house in the woods? The trust fund? My love?" But she just stared at me and later I told one of the workers and she said I must be mistaken. That there never was a child.

Not like that one anyway.

It must be the heat.

I don't know how to begin.

With the word harbinger maybe.

Or the sound of darts.

I can start with that.

All of my life whistling towards me.

φ

He texted me one April, back when I still had The Things of This World and was living somewhere Own-Roofed, a shaky place though, that last one, and I was getting older so quickly. I hadn't written about him in quite some time. Not in public anyway. Not since *The Book of Hymn*. He had been proud then at being my adored protagonist.

"This is me, truly, how it was anyway. You really captured that time, Shea, so crazy, beautiful even."

"Did I?" Rarely could I look directly at him or I would think things, feel dumb hope.

"Yes. So. Thanks."

He may have said this. There was never any proof.

And did he cradle the pages? Wet snow around them in the darkness and he aglow for a moment with being known, at least in the Realms of Art.

The book had even been received by this podium, that plaque. For a time I was the NEO ROMANTIC, UBER INTELLECTUAL LYRICIST of a new generation. I made them hurt and ponder. Or cry and revolutionize. Something like that.

This had begun to irk Hymn eventually. How could Shea use his life to make herself a kind of fame?

"I never expected this," I explained.

"It doesn't matter."

"Intention does."

"No, only consequence."

"I fell in love with you."

"No excuse for this, this life-sucking you do."

He could be cruel, as all muses are.

But the text had sent me knee-jellied, shudder-gutted down.

His new girl had found the book, the girl he had left his wife for.

And I was pathetic or a hag now. A hag of lust, a sorry sack of word-flesh leaching from the unreachable fount. Sad.

He didn't say these things to me. But he did write:

"She isn't impressed."

"I told her nothing."

"Your book says it all."

"So?"

"It follows me everywhere."

"It is art, not life!"

"Now she likely thinks we had a grand passion, that we were soul mates or something."

"How terrible is that?"

"Bad for me."

"O, will I drive pussy away from you with the honouring of my opus?"

"You aren't that powerful. Just. Stay away now ok. I am tired of dealing always with this outfall. Did my wife not suffer enough? Please. Don't contact me again."

Did he write these awful endings?

He may have. There is no proof of this either now.

But from there on there was something that retreated and the Endless Unravelling began.

φ

There had been a Going Back since that time.

Shea watches the world revert from her perch by the Golden Holy Pawn Shop where she clutches the signifier of her participation in society: a Starbucks cup. It is better than ID. Shea figured this out during her first week on the street. If you carry the cup, no matter how mad or unwashed you look people will think you have money. Best if it is a grande cup with your name scrawled on it in black felt. Never use the cup to beg though and make sure it is always at least half-full of any kind of liquid so you can pretend to sip its contents as you stroll.

"Out for a toddle?" is what they say to her when she leaves her room in the Permanent Emergency House or "Going downtown for a bit?" because she usually alternates between strolling Columbine Street, her allotted strip of asphalt, and taking up her post by the Golden Holy where she watches as many hours of the light as she can. There's a fairly roomy bench there, a skinny plot of flowers of some kind. A good seeing-things spot.

The Going Back had put her here maybe. On the street first, then into the Perm Emerg Home with the Idylls. Shea was supposed to be grateful for this rescue and for her cot & dresser combo with a loo down the hall and all those loopy neighbours. But her Pittance covered it at least. And she was close to Hymn's restaurant, even if one of the conditions of her stay was that she steer clear of its vicinity. Now even thinking about the past is just a habit really.

φ

Once Shea had lived in a Together House. It had slow velvet curtains and a mahogany table that extended and extended until it could seat a whole minister's cabinet or an army or even a choir with the basso profundo at one end and the nightingale at the other; it also had knick-knacks, memorabilia, souvenirs, gee-gaws and a steamer's trunk to keep her secret things in. Sepia photographs of noble ancestors square-danced on the walls and a profusion of plants jungled about in the solarium. Was Shea raised there?

She recalls as much, this being the original manse of her heart and the many other places she inhabited too before the Unravelling into the hands of the Idylls—though instead of pattern there was usually chaos at the core. The velvet curtains she had in her other homes were soiled or only velour or they stank of Value Village. The table was just IKEA particleboard and her doo-dads were objects she often threw at the retreating backs of a panoply of men.

Even though one of them had married her, good and proper as her now-dead mother had sniffed, Shea knew all along how ephemeral this Pretty Time was going to be. It wasn't hers, you see; she hadn't made it. Not really. At the centre of her being she only made poems. And these are hard to live in, however richly draped and ripely furnished they are.

φ

"Shea," said The Husband one day after they had been married about nine or so years.

"What?"

"I can't take this anymore."

"What?"

"You have to go. I need to be alone."

"What?"

"It's too much. You are too much."

"What?"

"The way you are. You and your muse-hunger, your poem-lust. You won't change. I know this now. And you shouldn't have to maybe. But I can't either. And I'm tired."

This part is true. How it went. He the crisp customer, the master of his emotions, drawing all the lines in their long crumbling Sand Home and she a stupid fish, bubbling Wut Wut Wut because she couldn't understand why the way she was in the world was always wrong, unsupportable, rejected, inevitably beyond endurance.

And now her Lovely had dwindled, it was easier for The Husband. He could take his leave, seek Normal, repeat to all, I tried, I really did but Shea had Freedom stuck in her Cortex and she wouldn't stop her Spur of the Moments, her Boltings, Lungings, Ecstasies, Muse Seekings, Strange Amorousnesses, and Other Categories of the Impossible for the Societal Saint to turn a Blind Eye to. Anymore.

Shea had never saved. She stopped going to work. Quickly, the Unravelling began.

φ

Detrital, I.

φ

I did have an Appropriate Job once. With Regular Hours, a small but Consistent Paycheque and thus some pride in telling people at the Right Kinds of Parties that I was an Agency Worker.

It doesn't matter what agency. Nor what I did. There were stacks of paper, clicking computers, file folders, a water cooler and I was generally concerned to Impress the Boss who sat in his swivelling leatherette chair with faux diplomas on the wall, sniffing at my credentials. Joyce worked there too and Alan and Kate. People from a Past Life now.

It was where I first met the Muse. Hymn worked across the street as a Factory Operator, then with clipboards, grinding machinery, walkie-talkies, chemical fumes and less need to Impress the Foreman who stomped around in his white hard hat barking random orders.

"Not to worry. I will come into money soon," was how Hymn had phrased it, his hope for the future, when they had started chatting one afternoon over bagels at Sal's (mine a humiliation of poppy seeds, his a clean plain circle of dough), "and then I will open my restaurant."

Hymn is Greek, well his family is, and solid, tall, flashingly dark as the cover hero on one of her mother's Harlequin novels but sharper, musical, much more glazed with alluring reticence than unbuttoned beguiling.

I wasn't drawn to Hymn right away.

With Epic that had happened. An instant shlurp gulp and gone. As if he had a vacuum vortexing in his eyes. I didn't have a choice I kept telling the Husband.

But Epic was dead long since.

By his own hand, the papers had written, as if he had snatched himself up as a hawk does with a field mouse and cast his body down on the Hard Evermore of his not being here.

I had only the pale books I had composed from his twisted beauty, his tortured gorgeousness.

The Husband nearly left me then. But I made promises. I Settled Down. And by Hymn's appearance I wasn't as given to imagining the Sweet Ease, the Plentiful Emptiness of Muses. So I steeled myself, became some other material that caught the sun but was not scarred by it.

For a while.

φ

He booted me out. The Husband did. Took the little we had, shunned me. I couldn't work at the agency anymore then. Did I tell you this? And a woman over fifty has no chance to be viewed as anything other than the erosion of possibility. I still had my books though. And so I stomped over to the Room of Assistance with the stack of them and when the Drab took me in I plonked the weight on her desk and barked:

"Do these mean nothing?"

"What are those, pray tell?" she snorted.

"Why books. My books. The books I wrote. All eighteen of them. Some even won awards once," and I pointed out the fading gold crowns and stars on the covers to her dull gaze.

"Why would this matter now, Number 386, when you need assistance from us?"

"Well, because... I gave my life to this vocation, my job was always uncertain, I have no medical, no retirement, I signed no agreement with the Husband, we owned nothing really and to write those books, many of them, I had to well... nourish my Muses."

"I have no idea what you're talking about."

"It's just, I could never be only with one... person... the writing demanded... I know others... passionately... get obsessed so to speak... in a kind of madness to compose."

"So you cooked your goose to sum it up."

"What?"

"Obviously nothing you have accomplished has benefitted your long-term existence."

"What about these? Books!"

Drab stared at me with her dry mind browning as if I had placed a mound of petit-point embroidery before her in carefully worked scenes of eighteenth-century farm life.

"Yes, but where is your income?"

"I told you! Is this all that matters?"

"Here, yes. As an assister, my only job is to determine your worth to society."

"Is the writer not valuable, a kind of sage, even historically speaking, god-like?"

"Maybe Ancient Peoples thought this way, Number 386, but who reads now? I hear libraries are ditching books by the millions and you can't compete with Happy Screens now can you?"

"No! Books will always be crucial. I refuse to believe otherwise! Books are holy monuments to the senses and the imagination. Essential for the human heart."

"Truly I see no proof. Now good day."

And with that, Drab slammed my file shut, assigned me to Nil.

φ

It happened like an unbearably lovely illness. The Slipping. One day Shea could sustain the Routine Job, the Husband. She was even growing a lemon tree on the patio and every morning felt its fragile need as a necessary anchor. Gently, she had resigned. There would never be another Epic. Sadly relieved Shea was, sorrowfully lightened. The H and her had even gone for a picnic that last Saturday morning on the Isle of Crowe, a real spread: artichokes, braised pear salad, harvest bread, old cheeses, cured meats and chilled wine. All laid out upon one of those nostalgic tablecloths. In a field thick with flowers no one had planted, unbidden and delicate.

"Shea," the H had said, even taking her hand (they were already in their later forties, married eight years, it wasn't a required gesture), "I'm proud of you."

"Why hon?"

"You've become so much calmer, stable. Maybe those Times of Upheaval are beyond us, eh."

"Seems that way. I told you as I got older it would get easier."

"Yes, but at times I didn't know if I could wait for the Subsiding. Now I think, most days, it was worth it."

"Good." She had bit hard into a gherkin and felt all her flesh sigh into this comfort, this security.

Then, that night, that very evening, she had seen Hymn play his guitar at the Muse Bar and was done for again.

φ

The Muse Bar was the place the edgy bands played and on Fridays they hosted an open mic for local artists. Over their bagels the week before, Hymn had told her that he and two other guys from the Factory had a group called Rime and that this would be their first show. Would she come?

Of course she would.

But how to tell the H?

"Hey, wasn't Epic a musician too?"

"Yes. So? This is totally different, dear."

"You have a thing for guitar guys though, don't you."

"That is not why he was my Muse. I didn't even know he played when I met him, remember?"

"Sadly, all too well."

(The chaos of this instant and yet its utter clarity. How leaving H at the party and walking into the darkness with Epic six years ago had felt perfectly right, as if there was no other choice, and when the poems came, vindication of this action for her, if not for those who live Outside of such Impulses, including the H.)

"So don't you think if this was going to happen again it would have already?"

"Maybe."

"I mean we chat pretty regularly over bagels and nary a poem yet."

"Bagels aren't poetic."

"Anything can become poetry."

"Nah, I will never believe that. Well, be safe."

And thus he had Given his Blessing. He wasn't Insensitive; he had Endured. But there was something about her that offended his Rational Heart, his Logical Mind. It was evident by then and eroding fast.

φ

At the Perm Emerg Home run by that Vast Troop of Idylls, only one man understands her now: the Rose-Gardener. Unlike the others who slop around in baggy sweats and tees emblazoned with miniature cats and ball caps stuffed onto their stringy mops, the RG sports a faded brown suit with natty black shoes and still slicks his hair back with Brylcreem. And he seems to listen to her when she talks, even as he clips and prunes his beloved flowers.

Shea doesn't often ask why the Others are in Perm Emerg and the Idylls forbid even the sharing of last names but with the RG she is more comfortable. He had heard voices; this was what put him here years ago. The voices had told him he was the Grand Magus and could save the universe if he conjoined with Bloody Betty the burlesque dancer and they went on a Purification Rampage with glowing pitchforks. Needless to say, his wife hadn't agreed to his plan and BB got him thrown in jail for the way he stalked her at the Red Balloon Nightclub, but fortunately no Rampaging with farm implements had ever been undertaken and when he arrived at Perm Emerg some twenty years back they had put him on a Giant Corps Drug that had kept him docile. Then he'd discovered roses.

φ

It had always seemed to Shea, those nights she spent watching Hymn at the Muse Bar, his band Rime becoming regulars on their roster, that it was her and only her who had been selected—by whom—as his designated recorder, depicter, adorer. His wife had never gone to shows and after he left her and got the girlfriend, a worthy trinket undoubtedly, so much younger than her, trimmer, always stylish and given to quoting poetry for effect in Webland, well she went, but was never to be found at the front of the stage, stirring her lithe body to the music or even snapping photos. No, his Arm Candy stayed always within her circle of women friends—chatting, giggling, huddling off to one side like a clump of velvety, irrelevant blooms. The AC would tip her pretty head at Shea in passing, all smiling politeness, but Shea had often caught her glancing disdainfully at the way she couldn't help but stare at Hymn, at the hundreds of pictures she took at his concerts and how her stockier body never stopped finding his rhythm as he played his guitar with those elegant electric hands. Only once had those fingers passed against her flesh, just once in the months he was between the wife and the AC. But somehow they had never ceased burning into her. It was stupid. It was delicious. Shea didn't want to remember this, the over and over of what was, years ago now, and never ever would it happen again.

φ

When they marked NIL on my file at Assistance after the H pointed his Righteous Finger at the door of our once somewhat-merry home and I walked away from one illusion, then another and I was left with Naught except the Once Was, the Idylls didn't find me for quite some time. There was first a Wandering About and finally all I could think of was to enter the Muse Zone, the Residue of Muse Realm anyway, and set up camp near the man who had not addressed himself to me for so long, a year maybe, since the AC found The Book. He much younger after all and a Fine Upstanding Owner now, likely humiliated to have had this greying, shifting into paunch, gutted of fertility Beast Woman writing about his life, the evidence Evermore in those Useless Books, the one on Hymn even emblazoned with a gold orb, planet of acceptance.

He hadn't seen me then, what I was becoming, but I knew him well enough to sense him cringing from a distance, partly from guilt, partly from arrogance, tinged, I still wanted to hope, with affection. Yet this didn't stop me from setting up a camp bed beneath the copious ivy in a vacant lot down the road from Athena Taverna on Iris Avenue. What did I have to lose now? What would stop me from steeping wholly in my Muse without the love of my H and my home to hold me even if he would never reciprocate my desire? What was left me but this opening of myself to nothing?

φ

How had it happened, that once. She wants to tell the RG. Of course, the H had known. Eventually. Not the details, those exquisite, lurid moments. But just that Shea had gone from being workmates with Hymn and his watcher at shows, to being lovers, so briefly, and that this night, along with her "Damned Imagination" as the H called it, had made poems and poems and then a book that trumpeted itself into the world on its shameful bugle of "such a moving testimony to impossible longing" et cetera, et cetera. Hymn, yes, had been awkwardly proud at first, then after the girlfriend, made the equation and things got a bit difficult between them for a time, he had begun the Spurning. And her H told her to go then, that was when he had Endured Enough, when she had become Finally Insufferable. Why was it that men could so often hold onto both, a wife and a muse, while women had to be utterly chaste, owned, if they wanted to even come close to Ensuring a Modicum of Security? Shea, younger, had been fiercely determined that Nothing would Impede her Art and if given the Ultimatum, would always choose it before Safety. And old, older anyway, she guesses she has. This is what she has done. (The RG continues to clip at his adored tea roses. She's not sure he has heard a thing.)

φ

Shea wakes to rain, a downfall that ticks and clacks on the tarp she has draped over the camp bed through the slim shield of the blackberry and salal that arches over and spreads around her.

This is her routine during The Lost Time: a morning pee, throw another layer of clothes on (flowing tunic, over-sized cardigan, stretchy pants), walk down to the Gospel House for some eggs and white toast on a paper plate and a Styrofoam glug of coffee and then take up her Post behind the Taverna, in the parking lot's hedge on the other side of the Gladioli Garden.

She is usually there by lunch hour. He never sees her. Though once he must have told his bus boy to clear out the old rags in the back bushes because the young man with nervous glittery eyes had crouched down to grab at her and let out a yelp when he realized the rags were animated. He hadn't told on her at least. "Shhhh," she had hissed at him as softly as she could, "I'm just doing my own thing is all. Don't worry about me ok." A jittery nod and he was off to grab ice cream wrappers off the clematis.

Shea has done this for months, this daily ritual. Watch Hymn pull up in his BMW, sometimes with the AC, and enter the tavern, all suit and smooth and strong-backed, though at night (she sees this through the windows once it gets dark), he unbuttons a bit, gets tousled, laughs himself to sweet creases as he plays guitar for the ouzo drinkers, the tzatziki scent wafting over her until Shea imagines, hungry as she is, that she will be cooked up next, all her flesh suf-fused with sauces and animal smells, leftovers she claws out of bags from the dumpster.

It is enough just to be near him somehow.

φ

They had gone for a drink that long ago evening, following one of his concerts. He had already opened the taverna; Shea was still working at the Agency but had recently sold a short story to *Ploughshares*, a poem cycle to *Poetry Chica-go*. Perhaps she was finally on the up and up, whatever that meant, but Hymn was impressed anyway. She always knew he needed youth, beauty to nourish his longings or if not those, then some fame at least shuddering around the objects of his desire. Now others wanted her, he did too, however momentarily. And the wife was gone; the AC not yet available, though he was never without female admirers. Shea was the only one who came to all his shows though, despite her H's objections. Was it desperate? To others it appeared so (she understood this later) but to her, being present for everything she could was essential to what she was writing, a low flame of poems that would flare up and sear out of her after that one night.

"Why are you always here?" he said to her once.

"To see you. I enjoy the music. And supporting what you do" (downplaying, as always, the intensity of her ache).

"Not that I don't appreciate it but..."

"I get it. I don't have to if you..."

"No, don't get me wrong..."

But that time he had bought her wine and three or four shots of Jager and Shea had felt herself becoming luminous beyond her years, less anxious, able to look Hymn in the eye and smile and be witty. And they had ended up in the scrubby local park with its few swings, a small vegetable garden, a string of oak trees, beneath which he had slipped into her in the shadows, those fingers intense upon her face and fast she had found herself crying out against his hard, warm stomach. Afterwards, walking her back to the train, he was both tender and strange and she knew that would be the only time he would ever yield to her.

ϕ

In the end, delirium took me.

I forgot to return to the camp bed and eat at the Gospel House.

Instead, I would just fall asleep in the hedge with shit and garbage around me and wake only wondering where Hymn was.

Then I got sick.

And my coughs brought the bus boy back.

This time he called the Enforcers.

And so the Idylls got me and did he know?

I couldn't tell by then who knew what.

At any rate, he didn't come running after me to offer me a roof with him and his darling.

No, how could he even claim to know me, if he had known.

φ

Months later and Shea stands beside the Rose Grower as he prunes the twinings of thorns down the wire fence outside Perm Emerg. The Idylls leave them be while she watches him garden, at least until dusk. But she can't touch the browning petals. He won't let her. "Do I write your poems for you?" he had snapped once when she had loosened a crumbling bloom.

"Well no…"

"Then…"

"It isn't the same, RG, c'mon!"

But soon she had grown silent, realizing that for the RG it was and would Shea have ever let this man, the only one she can now trust, squat beside her in the hedge and stare at her Muse, never mind make something, a thing of art, from Hymn?

The Idylls won't even let her walk past the Taverna now. If she leaves Columbine Street and heads away from the Golden Holy there is an alert sent to the Enforcers. Iris Avenue isn't good for her. It is written on her Charts.

"Thanks for just letting me watch eh," she tells the RG, the two of them Together-Alone in the world with the mute, beautiful flowers and the unappeasable ineffability of their singing.

The Muse-Eaters of Moosonee

Men had to keep an eye out for them. They had to stay wary. Never let their guard down. The poets were everywhere! (Or, in Russia, the poetesses.) They were dying in droves. The men that is. Or so the news bulletin is reporting, front page, bold lettering, a plethora of exclamations: "Men of Canada! Look out! An underground coven of female poets is suspected of the cruel seduction of countless men with the SOLE AIM of turning them into MUSES! These she-beasts have no morals, no conscience. All they want is to WRITE POETRY, and if it means the sacrifice of your son, brother or even husband, they are READY! These literary witches are unstoppable!"

Deandra Jackson, sitting at her kitchen table in Moosonee, reads on.

Apparently, the methods of these killer poets have been studied thoroughly. First, through the clever insertion of secret cameras into their urethras during routine Pap smears. These tiny gadgets track every nasty attempt to plunge their victims into the wet depths of their fleshy traps. Then, their journals and letters have been "recovered and analyzed by both a convent of nuns and a bevy of rednecks for evidence of illicit acts and vegetarianism." Finally, the poetry of these vile termagants have been parsed by a subversive team of illiterates who specialize in boiling poems in vats until they have extracted the minuscule evil meanings they are looking for, the gist that remains after the obliteration of such unnecessary elements as metaphor, irony and all other subtle or otherwise multilayered options for interpretation.

From these incontrovertible sources, researchers have "proven that poet after poet follows the same course of action: Pick em, Poke em, Prod em and POOF! Or in layman's terms: Victim selection, Victim luring, Victim torture and Victim dispatch. Men are simply not safe anywhere they go. That gorgeous blonde eyeing them as they sip their innocent coffee or beer? SHE COULD BE ONE OF THEM! And BOOM, if he lets himself just once slip into her iambically-tantalizing grasp, IT WILL BE TOO LATE! Driven mad by lust for her deceptive beauty, tormented by her decided incapacity for monogamy and worked into a frothing frenzy by her relentless production of poetry, the man WILL HAVE NO CHOICE but to commit suicide by taking the JU-JU pill (available through Jackson & Jackson in powdered, injectable or smokeable forms, depending on individual predilections).

At least it would be set up by these hellish sonneteers TO LOOK LIKE SUICIDE, but in fact it is MURDER! MURDER BY POEM IN THE FIRST DEGREE!!!

Deandra harrumphs to herself but decides to keep reading to the end.

"These brutal bards may APPEAR to be mourning the loss of the men they once deviantly drew into their poetic webs, but in actuality, they are gleeful. A MUSE, A MUSE! They cackle rabidly in their sewer-deep dens, before setting out to write their award-winning, top-selling, Hollywood-producible books of poems about those NOW-DEAD MEN! Shocking, I know, but IT'S ALL TRUE! These poor victims' lives don't matter at all to the versifiers of DOOM. No, they are willing to endure every form of agony and inflict all manner of pain just TO GET A POEM OUT OF IT!"

Ok, ok, that's enough, Deandra says out loud, slapping the paper down on the table. They've got it all wrong. Men don't have to be dead to give us poems! Au contraire, the longer we can keep those muses alive, the more books of verse we can churn out from their capacity to inspire us regularly in our day-to-day lives. As long as, she adds, they're kept on a rather short leash.

"Right, Harvey dear?"

Deandra smiles serenely, patting the balding head of a man tied tightly to one of her legs, then rises, dragging him, not even uncomfortably, across the floor to her desk. "Well," she sighs, clicking on her laptop, then gazing sweetly into his eyes, "it's time to get to work."

The Dead

The Man Who Came Back from the Dead

"Grief's an eclipse. It comes and it goes."
—Charles Wright

He returned on a Thursday. She had just washed her hair, and is now humming, for some stupid reason, that Scorpions tune he used to sing to her, "No One Like You." A day off from the warehouse and she twists her red locks tightly in a towel, wanting them to dry fast so she can step out on some errands: groceries, the post office, a pedicure maybe.

Then paint.

The canvases she is working on towards a showing next year of her memorial work: Elegy for Vince. Eight 30 x 40 paintings of her dead husband's face layered with clippings of articles on him she had once collected: "Perkins has a Bright Future in Hockey," "#12 takes the game with a Howitzer in the final minutes," "Once the Warrior's unbeatable power forward, Perkins has been spending a bit too much time in the Sin Bin this season, but promises to return with more Pretty Goals soon."

A stirring in the hall, a rustling sound around her front door mat, or is that a hesitant knock, improbable at this early hour, and how would they have gotten into the building anyway? She shuts off the bathroom fan, peers through the peephole. Yes, a man is standing there, that much is clear, slender, seemingly impatient, one of his legs jittering, hands tapping at his thighs. Somehow she doesn't recognize him at first but neither is he strange, like a memory transformed by art, a watery surfacing in the dark pond of her mind, and no it couldn't be.

She presses her eye closer to the hole.

"Vince?" How quavering with disbelief, with hope and terror, her voice suddenly is. She holds this apparition in its distorting fish eye a moment, then pulls back, blinking wetly.

"Yes, yes, of course it's me. For some reason my key doesn't work. A chick let me in below but she was fucking weird about it. What's up? Let me in, babes!"

So she turns the lock. Opens the door. Stands there silent while "hey hon," he dashes out then agitates past her into the kitchen. She can hear him yank open the fridge, scan the shelf for beer. She knows this is what he is doing as if her cortex has reshuffled the cards of her old life and placed this image foremost in her mind.

"Baby, didn't you get any Stellas?"

Of course, she wants to yell back, four years ago. Before they found you dead in your truck from an overdose. Yes, darling. Four years ago I bought you Stellas and you didn't even get a chance to drink them. But I did. I had four freaking years to down those cold ones.

This is what she wants to reply right now, a bitter sting throbbing in the back of her throat, her heart knotting itself in her chest like a terrible lesson in how to stay moored. How the? Why? Can this even be?

You don't do this, dead man.

Respond to the pleas of your loved ones and return.

Not after so many years of grieving when the body has only recently started to redraw its boundaries, to imagine a state of non-yearning for absence, to weep, to rage less often.

And to make art about what had happened.

That formerly rising hockey star Vince Perkins, she whispers to herself as if rewinding an old newscast, the man of promise who had gotten sucked into the wrong circle one lonely night when he was playing in Pittsburgh and utterly addicted to junk, dying within a year from the stuff, her power forward emaciated, unwashed, claiming he was still fine, totally, while their accounts were sapped and she was only his abstract anchor by then, the early desire between them muted, the trips to Mexico, their puppy he had named Puckface, the house they had bought in the Seattle 'burbs, all nothing nothing nothing.

What is she supposed to say to him?

This spectre rummaging in her fridge in the apartment they had never even lived in together.

How does he not realize he is dead?

She had claimed his body at the morgue, made arrangements for its cremation, taken the heavy box of ashes and buried it in the hockey players' memorial garden with a plaque: Vincent Michael Perkins (1982–2009). Always loved. Forever missed.

Was he going to explain his presence now, after four long years, by telling her it had all been a joke, that he had been hiding out in some coven for junkies, or maybe recovering in a secret treatment centre in the desert?

She inches across the wall and slides around the corner to the kitchen. His back is to her, bent over, muscles sketched through his thin shirt, one of his hard arms reaching behind the milk container, "Sweetheart, where have you hidden them, eh? I know you picked some up on Tuesday."

Is it Thursday still? Still 2013? She pulls her phone out of her pocket, checks quickly. Yes.

"Vince, please," she finds herself sighing out, "can you sit down?"

He shifts his head towards her with that tender furrow of forehead, one eyebrow cocked, "Um, ok... what's going on?"

Lets the fridge door fall closed. Perches on one of her bar stools. Places his spread hands on jeaned knees.

"Where have you been?" she starts off, her voice like water torn with nervous breezes. Barely able to glance at him, unable to move.

"What do you mean?"

"You've been gone a long time, sweetheart."

"Really... hardly... I don't think so... I mean what's long?"

"Like four years, honey."

She watches him slowly scan the rooms now: the new leather sofa, her easel in one corner, her assortment of cacti, the few photos on the mantel, one of the two of them in 2007 at the beach with Puckface, her with their nieces, then one of her with Eric, whom she has been seeing for a year now. They are kissing in the picture; it was Christmas, his office party, a glowing moment; she follows Vince's confused gaze.

"I don't know how to tell you this," she begins again.

He is looking at the painting she is in the middle of. A piece where his strong features are overwritten with slatherings of newsprint. Words like Hat Trick, Going for the Cup and In the Final Period seem to float over his tense lips, his scooped-out cheekbones.

"Nice," he says, but already his voice has lost that innocent joviality, has flattened into a vague flickering.

"Vince. Precious man."

"Yeah." And now he stares directly at her as if trying to absorb all he has returned for and yet the loneliness in his eyes persists, deepens. She is no longer connected to keys, Stellas, Tuesday for him, even affection, but is floating softly and painfully away into a place he rupturingly realizes he has never before entered.

And then she tells him,

"You're dead, my love. You died."

But Not Broken

His ashes. We can use his ashes you know. Mix them with the ink, Brian is saying to her. The tattoo shop is on Kingsway. The requisite laminated flash art, binders of designs on the glass-topped counter, a sterile, tiled feel punctuated by a Slayer soundtrack and the scratchy buzz of needles working on flesh.

Mia is holding his last card to her: roses, a heart, Valentine's Day. Just six weeks ago. "Cracked but not broken," it reads in his childish black printing, then, "Please still be mine. All love, your Jay," his signature a reaching loop pursued by a scrawl. Around a design she's sketched of a guitar entwined with a paintbrush. Mia wants these words. This her first tattoo. Probably her last. On her shoulder, down to her elbow on her right arm. *You just have to bring a small baggie of it, Ziploc. Do you want this?*

She does.

φ

They make an appointment for the next day. 2 pm. Mia goes home to the nothing-house. Where every object: Jay's Rickenbacher, his softened work shirts, his once-favourite blue clay coffee mug, even her easel, paints, the useless food in the fridge, the mocking early blooms on the lilac bush mean absence. A lack of connection. Loss of whatever made them resonate. She sits a lot with her head on the table, cheek pressed uncomfortably against the hard wood. Not even feeling this. Sighs like an old animal. Cries from a cavern of darkness, some ancient place of agony she didn't know she could access so readily and often. *Do you need anything?* People say this to her. Kayla, her best friend, who stays for hours brewing up cup after cup of tea. Ellis, her sister, dropping by with a mac and cheese, Jean from the centre with carnations. *I'm so sorry for your loss*, they tell her and some add, *if it was going to go on that way... after all... well it's better... in some sense... don't you think?* No, she wants to rage at them. Love doesn't want death under any circumstances, even the worst. But they can't possibly comprehend the connection she and Jay had forged over the past six years. And she is too exhausted even to reply. Just shows them her tear-yarded skin, the pale and blotchy canvas of it, and they are silent then. Nearly scuttle, after a brief embrace, away.

φ

The next day she's at the shop early, holding the bagged ashes in her hand, a grainy teardrop. She hadn't been able to think of what to do with his remains until the tattooist's suggestion and still, there is so much of Jay to deal with, this only a palm-full taken from the swollen hive of white, much finer than Mia had ever imagined, here and there the chunk of an unburned tooth fragment amid the powder of his lost flesh, that was all. She had carefully sifted those shards out, dropping each piece that had survived the cremulator into a baby food jar that had once held paint, yellow paint, flakes of it sticking to the glass like misplaced sunshine against the grey remnants. He'd never liked his teeth. Another irony. The front ones he thought were too big and then one of the side incisors was broken, an old hockey injury. Yet this is all that's left in any way recognizable from the man who was over six feet tall, sinewy, scruff-jawed, scraggle-haired, callus-handed, slow to smile, quiet and raucous by turn. This all. And memories of course, too many. Every time one splinters into Mia's mind, she winces, flinches from recalling the meals they served each other—he favouring the slow-cooked game hens, she the fast pizzas, their walks down the Fraser with Turbo, their collie, dead last year after lapping up anti-freeze in the neighbour's garage, and most of all, their collaborations when Jay was between long-haul shifts, he strumming his guitar as she painted her canvases, notes and colours flurrying together until his songs bore the titles: "Ochre Memory," "The Black Garden" and her acrylic works—*Melody in the Afterhours, Tunes beyond Ruins*. And their bodies, of course—him suspended above her, her eyes opening into his, that heat. God, too painful. The constant ache for it all to be erased. She places the ashes on the counter, calls out to Brian, wherever he is, *Here I am, I'm here.*

ϕ

How had it begun, his addiction? Mia still doesn't really know. Jay had always smoked, toked, drank a few beer when home from the road. On the weekends sometimes he'd get *shittered,* as he called it: Screwdrivers, Jager shots, but nothing seriously out of control. He never really got crazy when he was drunk. Laughed inanely instead, strummed his guitar at high speeds, talked rapidly. The next morning though, he would be dark, too quiet, slump in bed with the dog.

What's the matter, babes?

Nothing much.

Doesn't seem like that.

Well, yeah.

Look honey, if you're getting sick of the road, living here, whatever, we can change things, do something different.

Did I ask for that?

No, but...

Just forget about it then. It's nothing.

Their conversations would go like this on these kinds of days. And then, a few hours later, he would break out of his funk, say—*hey, what about a zombie movie and some pop tarts?* Then they would head to the studio where he would plug in, noodle a little, and Mia would feel her mind fill with textures, her hand reach for the tubes of paint, her brushes, and the flow of colours would begin. The most relaxing and yet productive moments she had ever known happened then. And their laughter, the looks that flew such soft birds between them. Easy to imagine after such sessions his gloom was nothing more than a hangover.

That October, she'd been accepted at Banff, the fall he became addicted to crack. Two whole weeks she would be able to work in the Leighdon Studios. Of course, she told him she was going.

φ

Jay would be off the road while she was gone. Such perfect timing. They rehearsed the litany of chores that needed to be done and when.

Garbage day?

Tuesday morning right now, babes.

Plants—any need special care?

Just the bonsai—remember—soak it for fifteen in the sink if it's dry.

How will I know?

Lift the pot. It'll be light.

Ok. Anything else?

Not a lot. The basics you know. The usual stuff.

Being alone on the highway was one thing for Jay, Mia sensed, and being home alone quite another. Like he lost his focus, got full of loose ends. Still, she didn't need this nagging anxiety, had to trust his ability to cope so she could make her paintings, not waste the brief time she had up there. He's a grown man after all. Regardless, she finds herself consoling him before she even leaves.

It's only two weeks, honey.

I know, yup.

And you can get some recording done, chill a bit without me ragging on you.

Ha. You bet. I'll be dandy. And hey.

What?

I'm proud of you, kiddo.

And so she'd breathed deeply, packed the car with blank canvases, tubes of paint, energy bars and a few bottles of wine, hugged him fiercely and set out.

φ

Brian's rubber-gloved hands slap a lozenge of Vaseline on Mia's shaved upper arm. He's already mixed several pinches of ash into the black ink with a tiny tool of some kind. Now he's laying the stencil of Mia's drawing upon her skin, lifting the tracing paper, leaving behind a purple outline of the guitar, paintbrush, Jay's words. She's starting to sweat, imagining the burn of the tattoo gun. Has been told it's like a bee sting, painful but cathartic. Good for grief.

How's it look to you?

Mia glances in the mirror. Quickly.

It's perfect, great.

Look again, ok. Is it straight? Right position? This is forever, you know.

She forces herself to stare longer, trying to abstract the image from her body, from the meaning of that inscription. Tears pop in heated beads into her eyes.

I know. It's… fine.

Ok, you can't go back after.

You can never go back on anything, can you?

Her voice feels clotted, a jumble of sounds. And now she pulls in her breath, tenses in anticipation. He looks sideways at her, nods, turns on the needle, bends against her flesh, begins.

φ

The first half week, when Mia calls Jay, he sounds tired, full of missing, resigned. Tells her he is hammering together a birdhouse. A big one.

Kind of out of season, isn't it?

Yeah, well it's something to do. Gotta keep the hands busy.

Then, on the fifth day, she phones and he doesn't pick up. She leaves messages. First: "Hey baby, guess you're keeping busy. I'm up to my ears in paint of course. Can totally imagine you putting a soundtrack to this one. Think you'll love it. Ok. I'll call back in a few." Third or fourth try: "Hey, getting worried now. This isn't like you. Are you sick sweetie? Only a couple more days and I'm home. Will try again when I'm on my way." But almost worse than this inexplicable silence, just before Mia heads off to Vancouver, canvases stacked in the back of the car, she actually reaches him.

Hey! What's up, babes? Why such a stranger?

What are you saying. Gotta life, don't I. Not just when you're home. Tons of shit going on.

Oh... ok, well... I'm heading home now. How are things?

Cool, cool, yup, sweet. No problem.

Jay's voice: rudely hyper, detached, cold. Putting down the phone, Mia shudders, doesn't know why really. Can't stop.

φ

For days after she returns, Mia can't figure out what's happened to Jay. He helps her carry in the canvases, jittery, buzzing, despite how skinny he seems, cheeks diving in on either side of his mouth. The house is dirty, the plants dried out, yet Jay seems unconcerned, aloof even, when Mia lets out a wail, "My ivy, baby, it's dead, what the hell!" He only shrugs, goes to lie down in his unwashed clothes, doesn't go back to work, won't let her see him naked as if he scarcely remembers he has flesh. Mia wonders if he's ill, gone crazy. There's a silence between them she can't bridge though. Before she would have confronted him if he was acting... strangely. Now, it's like there's no common language left. And then she starts noticing things are missing: from the kitchen, the jam room. Jay has excuses for all of it—he lent that one out, the other broke, is in the shop. But once the bounced cheques start arriving in the mail, each with a cancelled stamp on it and a sinkingly negative balance in his account, Mia can no longer endure his evasive answers.

You stole from your own bank account? Have you gone totally fucking mad? What's going on? Come clean right now or I'm walking!

Jay startles at this, something ruptures in him.

Yeah I have... a problem. A thing happened.

You're damn right you do, but what is it? How could you do this, to you, to us?

Drugs. Yeah... crack.

What!

Crack. I, um, did it while you were gone. And a bit before. A lot of it. Didn't, yeah... mean to.

And he trails off, the air around them, the glare she's giving him, all ice.

φ

They can't afford to send Jay to rehab though he does get on the waiting list for the program funded by the Teamsters' Union. A long waiting list. In the meantime, Mia makes plans for him to get away from the city, his dealer, whoever this is, he refuses to say. His high school buddy, Darren, lives in Cache Creek with his young family, had always been a straight-up kind of guy and when Mia explains their situation, is open to having Jay come and stay for a few weeks in exchange for, as he says on the phone, "yard work, stuff like that, no it'll be cool to see the dude and... sorry." By this point, Mia just wants him gone, out of her sight. The thought of him wrecking everything so fast for what, a stupid high, is making her sick. She can't touch him, can barely look at him. They slink around each other in the house; avoid each other's eyes. She needs desperately to purify their home, the one they struggled to get a down payment for three years ago, the one they own together and that she is determined not to lose. How she wants to make art in it again without constantly finding busted glass pipes, smelling the searing memory of the drug. She can barely kiss him before he boards the Greyhound, duffel bag in hand, guitar on his back, looking at her as he leaves like a lost child.

φ

Weeks later when he comes home, Mia scarcely recognizes him, he is so beautiful. Glowing. His skin, smooth and fed. His eyes, truly seeing her again. They hadn't talked much while he was at Darren's. She'd wanted distance, thought Jay should try to imagine life without her for those weeks and see how it went. Not even wanting to think about a future yet not willing to leave him yet. Apparently, and reassuringly, it has gone well. He has eaten, stayed off drugs, worked hard in Darren's yard. In the meantime, she has literally been cranking out canvases, black and white 11 x 14s, small intense squares of paint called *Rock #1*, *Rock #2* and so forth. She's painted seventeen by the time Jay comes back. She takes him by the hand now, brings him to the studio.

Look, baby.

He's silent for a long time.

Wow. He tries at last. *Is that what I did to you? Rough.*

No. It's what you did to yourself. Mostly anyway. Making these helped me get through all those days, wondering if I could stay, if you would… recover.

Well I did. He squeezes her paint-smudged fingers, suddenly rambling. *I'm better than ever and I will never let that happen to us again. I promise. Hell, sweetheart, I nearly croaked, thought my heart would bust just like that. Freaked me out. I don't want to lose everything. Don't want to lose you. It's not going to take us down. Don't worry.*

She is the quiet one now, staring at his brightness, taken aback by this new and purer energy. Feeling a difficult sense of hope.

And you know the first thing I'm gonna do so you know I'm serious? He looks at her intensely, then back at the paintings.

What?

I'm not afraid of what's happened. What you've made here. I'm going to compose music for these paintings, the whole damn series, and we'll perform it at the Gallery Café like we did in the past with other stuff. It'll be amazing. Everything will be like it was.

Jay suddenly punches his tanned fist through the air between them, *I'm back kiddo! Can't you see. It's ok.*

φ

Months pass. Jay has done what he said he'd do, composing seventeen agonized bluesy fragments of song that echo off her dark visions almost too accurately. Some audience members nearly weep when they perform it early in the year at the gallery, her paintings each glued at the bottom to a glass tube, then mounted with black wire, Jay perching on a spot-lit chair in their centre, just his Rickenbacher and a mic, strumming and crooning.

What a team you two are! Ellis had gushed after the show. *Seriously. Some kind of miracle-makers. Who says art can't save!*

Mia wants to believe this. But their art this time is mostly just a record of the agony they've both suffered. It's no guarantee he won't go back to the drug. What is helping, she thinks, is that she's taking care of their money, spending lots of time with him. They're talking more, making love softly, with such feeling. And Jay has said to her, keeps saying, *Baby, I almost died. You think I'd make that kind of mistake again? It was bad but now I'm over it. We gotta put it behind us. Move on.*

φ

The bright colours are slowly being ground into her skin. Those letters, each etched with the finest of needles, rising up into sharper focus against the blues and golds of the paintbrush, the guitar. The pain isn't bad. Bad enough to distract her from the other pain though. Now Mia can't pull her eyes away from the mirror, reading the backwards words as if they are comprehensible, reciting them from memory: "Cracked but not broken. Please still be mine. All love, your Jay." Each word ridged, almost bubbling up with ink as her eyes again tighten with tears. The bastard. The son of a fucking bitch. God how she hates him. Lying to herself right now is the only way she's able to feel anything resembling good. Anger always more bearable than a complete dissolving in a sorrow she isn't sure she will ever be able to recover from.

φ

The card, the Valentine's one, came after it had happened again. After it had happened again and she had left him and returned. Only a weekend of buying, hooting, pawning while Mia was in Seattle, shopping with Kayla. She returned with a cheap box of wine and some hot discount boots to find Jay already coming down off his binge, trembling on the living room rug. He cried when she said she was leaving. *O god, no, just, don't, no, you, please baby.*

Everything was leaking out of him. He was so bony again, so apologetic. It wasn't enough. She left yes, but just for the week, a few days. Stayed with Ellis because she was the most sympathetic. Kayla couldn't quite be there for her. "How could you even think of going back!" she snapped over the phone. Ellis said little. "Stay as long as you need," she told her. But Mia couldn't stop herself from taking Jay's calls. He had gone back to work, claimed he had nothing left to pawn. That his dealer was moving to Abbotsford and besides he would never forget the pain he was causing everyone again. Why did she believe this, want to? His voice was so raw, gruff with love. Then that card, roses. She meeting him at their favourite restaurant, Shine. And his face full of light once more. The aching in her to keep him like this forever.

φ

When Jay dies, Mia isn't away, but yes, they are apart. April 2nd. Over a month since she's returned. He's on the road once more. She never finds out who sold him his last hit but when he doesn't call that night or the next, she knows he's dead. "I'd like to file a missing person's report," she tells the officer over the phone. Data: 6 ft 2, 195 lbs or maybe less by now, thirty-three years old, brown hair, an old tattoo of a blackbird on his inner left wrist, scars of course, a dent in his forehead from a rock, cuts on his hands. Yes he is driving a rig for Transport Central, the route between Vancouver and Revelstoke usually, yes he left three days ago and should have been home already. Twelve hours of anxiety later and Mia calls back.

Have you found anyone, anything?

They put the chief of police on the line.

Yes ma'am, I believe we did, a rig on the side of the road beyond Celista, a body in it matching your description, can you head to the morgue as soon as you can for identification purposes?

This is not how such things happen in crime dramas. Don't the cops always come to your door to inform you in person: their burly chagrin, your sudden bawling, Kleenexes proffered. Et cetera. Instead, she is told over the phone, and at the morgue, rather than being able to touch him from the proximity of a slid out drawer, can only view Jay behind glass, his stone head swathed in a sheet, long body swaddled. The curtain whirs back and there he is, a strange Sleeping Beauty on a metallic dais. An autopsy had already been conducted. Mia decides then and there she doesn't want a report of the results; that she knows what happened. His heart, a clot or something, some disastrous overload and that was that. His effects in a plastic bag: ring, lighter, wallet, a photo of her stuck in the sleeve. Forms. Calls to a crematorium. The morgue director's hand enfolding hers in an oddly warm clasp, tears wracking her eyes with the most violent sorrow she has never imagined she could bear.

φ

Brian wipes down the tattoo and Mia glances at it one more time before he wraps it. The image stands out from the rest of her pale skin, a harsh yelling blotch of ink. At the moment, she loathes it, wishes it gone.

Not to worry. It will heal. Brian is saying to her.

I love it. It's fine. She replies flatly. So he lays gauze over it and then, tapes it up.

The Day of the Dead

Of course, he remembers Eduardo. How could he not, he of the avid erotic gaze and Eduardo only eighteen, a bellhop at the Hotel de la Soledad in Morelia with lips thick and sweet as *atole* and a picture of the Grim Reaper in his wallet, plasticized, fondled to softness, a prayer to the Virgin of Guadalupe on its back.

Yes, Eduardo had certainly been memorable.

But then too were so many other boys he had met on his travels to fifty-six countries and counting. One country for every year of his life, he muses, back home again in Milwaukee with his darling partner Dave or Puppy Two, tsk-tsking over him as he spills his soup, drips his coffee on their new caramel-hued carpet, so into his spreadsheets he is that, "You just can't seem to mind, can you," Dave's yanked-thin voice, "Now look, look, what's that, oh you've gone and done it again, naughty boy, naughty!" The exasperation Dave feels towards him is part of the glue of their relationship, Patrick knows, the strange delight he takes in commenting on Patrick's recklessness, his laissez-faire attitude to the details of things: tidiness, monogamy.

It's not that Patrick tries to worry Dave, needle him per se, it's just that irrepressible desire he has to muck things up a bit, then bask in Dave's gentle but ragged scolding. Time and time again. They've been together twenty years after all; Patrick can't imagine what would sever their bond at this point, if it hasn't happened over his slopping a Corona on Dave's laptop or his sleeping with Rohan, John, Colin, Jim or Mr. Costa Rica with his buns of milk chocolate steel, he has a hard time fathoming what would.

Not that Dave hasn't had his own little dalliances, but they've been fewer, further between, precise alignments of limbs, cleverly planned assignations with no drops wasted, no hearts wrecked. Patrick hasn't quite managed to avoid drama, he even courts it on occasion, taking up with his married boss, the hot letter carrier, and once a punk junkie he met panhandling in the town square, paying him for a blow job only to find he couldn't get rid of the kid afterwards. The punk had fallen in love with him for Chrissakes, to the point of camping out on his buff suburban lawn, begging him for an overnighter. Right there, in Primsville? Dave had merely shaken his head at him, snipping: "Now Number One Pup, he's got to go and pronto!" And so Patrick had called the cops, had the boy removed in cuffs for disturbing the peace. Still, nothing had shifted Dave's commitment to him; nor his really, what after all did wee affairs matter beside his long and weighty relationship with Dave? Until the Day of the Dead trip that is.

φ

The girl and he had been on the same tour, an intimate cavalcade of American sightseers intrigued by the continued rituals of mourners on the island of Janitzio. For Patrick, it hadn't been so personal, this trip; he could have chosen any number of other tourist adventures: hiking in the Andes, seal hunting in Iqaluit. This last-minute group had snagged him by promising a single room, free margaritas the first night and a higher likelihood of boy-watching opportunities.

Yet the girl, Arabella was her name, Patrick sensed right away, had private motivations for being on the tour. Oh, who was he kidding, he hadn't sensed this, as if he was that observant, of women anyway, she had, in fact, told him. On the third day of the week-long sojourn, they were sitting drinking beers on the plaza, just the two of them, the remainder of the group having opted for a shop at the House of Handicrafts instead, when she had pulled the picture out of her frayed copy of *Under the Volcano* (Arabella was one of those tourists, it was evident, Patrick thought, who travelled little but when they did, it became an obsessively nerdy pursuit in which each sight had to be matched with its related text, then the connections chronicled at length in a lined, wire-bound notebook).

A troupe of darned cute drummers had just plonked themselves in front of the *calavera* stall across from their table; there was a Chewbacca wandering about and clumps of children painted up like miniature Catrina dolls dashing from sucker to sucker, pointing at their plastic jack-o'-lanterns and jabbering on about needing pesos. Then Arabella had slid the picture from her book and Patrick had been done for. "This was my boyfriend," the girl announced, quite flatly, crisply. "He died. At twenty-seven. In a car accident." She had paused to let these details sink in as she watched Patrick absorbing the photograph, then she continued, "That's why I'm here."

Patrick scarcely heard her, snared as he was by the picture of this young man: his night-coloured curls, sleek skin, slender body, no doubt otter-slick, one hand lifting a coffee mug as he stood on a balcony somewhere: autumn bright trees in the background, the curve of a deck chair rising up by his slim hip. "Well now," he managed, "such a shame. Isn't he a hottie!" Thinking to himself absurdly, "Why her, you didn't want her, you want me, why not me." And he had kept staring at the photo as she fed the air more stories of his loss, murmuring to no one, "What a doll. An angel from heaven. Truly. Cute as pie."

He hadn't been able to stop thinking about the picture of the dead boy the remainder of the trip, peering over Arabella's shoulder every time she drew the photo out from that infernal book, recanting the words, if the person spoke Spanish, as most did, "Me Amor Muerte." He even dreamed about the kid. One night they were naked in bed together, he crooning to the lad as he entered him, sliding his fist up and down the boy's ridiculously tumescent cock, "You're not really dead, are you, no you just pretended you'd died to get away from her and now you're mine, all mine." He was out of control.

The last day in Patzcuaro, he could scarcely even look at Arabella, the boy was on his mind so often. Heck, he even passed up a chance to watch the studly copper workers of Santa Clara del Cobre, preferring instead to sit on the roof of the B & B by the flower market and soak in the sun of his futile reveries. The following morning, when the girl went to pay her bill for all the fruit salads she had consumed during *desayuna*, Patrick took the opportunity to slide into her room, scanning it rapidly until he located the book. He leafed through it fast to find the picture. Finally it popped out at him between pages 204–205. He briefly caught the words: Kubla Khan, Consul, neurasthenia and ei ei ei ei before he'd tossed it back where he'd found it, passing the photo under his shirt, into his waistband. Then he'd bid Arabella a rushed farewell before she suspected the photo's absence, and flew home to Milwaukee two hours later with that bewitching picture now stuck into the one book he'd brought with him, the New and Revised Edition of *The Wealthy Barber*.

Ei ei ei ei. He sat on the plane, justifying his theft to himself, "What kind of person reads such silly things. Not the type of woman this boy needs. I can tell just from looking at this photo that he's a math man, a guy who works with his hands, and a sweet and yielding lover to boot. Yowza." For he only spoke of the dead boy in the present tense now, telling Dave when he arrived home that this had been one of his fleeting conquests in Janitzio, a fellow tourist, bi, another delicious but dismissable fling.

Dave knew better though; hadn't they been together for twenty years and why did Patrick keep thinking he could fool him? "This is more than a crush, Peppermint Patty," he razzed him at first, then, "Why I believe you're in love with this kid, Puppy One!" It was terrible. At least he could be honest with Dave when he was asked if he was in touch with him, if he and the boy kept in contact. "No," he'd sigh, as if crestfallen, leaving out the dreams he continued to have where he and the beautiful man were both young together, frolicking freely in their perfect skins, so far from the wreckages of age, the tedium of suburbia, the blood and ravages of accidents, the eternal cold of the grave.

A Pot of Coffee

It still hadn't been two hours. Since she'd made the coffee that is. Or the timer would have beeped, the brew gone luke-warm. So strange, time. Seemed like she'd been crying for days and yet the coffee hadn't even grown cold, nothing had changed at all but the hierarchy of the tragedy. Again. Often, and with much more regularity than at first, the basic im-penetrable fact, "He's dead," would dominate in her brain, an uninteresting, overly obvious statement, easy to detach from. This thought announced itself several times a week or more, usually accompanied by either the banal shud-der of, "So terrible," or a deeply resigned, "How could it be otherwise." Either way, oddly enough, the impact of the announcement was similar on her emotions, a flatlining, the grim survivalist gritting of her psyche's teeth, a going on.

Today, however, she had slept in, woken at the awkward hour of eleven, made that coffee, automaton with the brute combatancy of her dreams and then—what had prompt-ed this shift—this sudden reordering of the grief hierarchy so that instead of generalizations she could access details, those protective declarations like, "He's dead," dropping to the bottom of the apex and surfacing instead, one memory or another, sharp, hard to endure with its assault on her senses, cruel with pointless beauty. Take this morning's in-vasion for instance. She recalled, out of nowhere, the last play they had gone to—*Don Juan* done by a puppet theatre company from Winnipeg—and how, before the doors had opened, the two of them had walked hand in hand to the little bar attached to the community centre. He had bought them both wine in overly tiny glasses and then, for some reason, an orange, or was it a mandarin, plucking it from a basket by the till, rolling it in his palm. The fruit had a small sticker on it, "Little Sweetie," it said and when they had sat down to sip their wines he had unstuck it from the skin and touched it to her cheekbone, saying, "This is what you are," laughingly. She had been prone to mocking any diminutives applied to her, or compliments for that matter, but he had been so happy to be alive at that moment, and that the two of them were still together after everything, that she hadn't done so. Mocked or laughed. No, she had smiled back at him instead, left it on her face throughout the show. And now this detail, revisited like an awful punchline, was what had been making her cry for hours. Or so it seemed. How he would never live again and yet the coffee was still hot, soothing her with its part in her daily routine. How could this be—it should be cold by now, this grieving that had gone on so long and why couldn't she just finally leap from the balcony, take all this tired hierarchy of pain with her, break it on the yielding cedar trees by the parking lot, make it equivalent and irrelevant and done, done, done.

A Guy, a Girl & a Ghost: An Homage to Marie Claire Blais's Three Travellers

"So time enters the work in two ways... No—it enters the work in three ways, the third being the time of a haunting."—Lisa Robertson (*Nilling*)

The woman stands on the edge of the bridge railing. It has been snowing in the way it does where she was born, each flake vanishing fast into the chilled but iceless waters of the river. There are hands reaching up to catch every flake, winter moths evaporating into the creosote sweat of the smallest palms in the world. She knows this railing well. Has held onto its divots and rust, the map of encrusting spreading over a once-regal orange, the metallic span that has crossed the river since 1898, a pre-war leap between cities. Always her city has been trying to elude its history and falling dark prey to its ghosts.

Moment One

That *indefinable feeling of age* Emily sensed in herself had finally accumulated now, this midden of years suddenly gathering its poisonous bouquet together, the courtier of loss bowing, presenting her with the incontrovertible proof of her ancient state.

"Don't talk like that!" Michael says, sitting beside her in the velvet emptiness of the concert hall.

What had she said? Now that she didn't know the difference between speaking and silence, the living and the dead, it was hard to negotiate relationships. He wouldn't understand.

"Just a weight," she began as if her tongue had broken, "a... dragging out... herded towards... I mean... Michael, can you hear the music?"

The auditorium, it is true, was void of people but rich with musk and gilded putti and dust and a long red carpet ran down the centre of Emily's heart like a luxurious scar.

Her ghost had marched down it to such uproarious applause because he had composed this piece after all; the program she didn't hold in her shaking hands proclaimed: "'Dark Night, Evermore: An Ode to Poe's The Raven' by James Blanchford."

"I am trying to hear what you hear," is what Michael replies, the strain on his face evident, an anxious planet tipped towards nothingness.

"I am sorry I keep taking you to these performances." Though she isn't apologizing really, thinking love should attend as many of the eulogies, symphonies and circuses presented it or else what was courage, endurance, the bond worth between those still alive who had converged at the site of pain?

"You aren't..."

"No."

"So..."

"Well, maybe, yes, sometimes."

"In what sense?"

"Just that it has to be so endless, shifting, but regardless, sorrow and you are..."

"I am?"

"Done, as you have said, with elegy."

Suddenly Michael, the living, fleshed, substantial man was a sack of absence, lips gaped, hands limp, scarcely a person, barely breathing, while on the gutted stage, James was bright in his invisibility, a spectre so present with love, his piano glowing as he made the music she could not translate for anyone, really.

Sunday

Once upon a time there was no Michael. Or he was only a shadow of little relevance. Emily would hear that he, among many other pale names, was acting in a production of Sartre's *No Exit* or Beckett's *Waiting for Godot*. About ten years ago he had written and performed in a play called *Gut* but Emily hadn't seen it.

James was alive then, tearing her mind up with his songs, making her sing with him in soprano agony because he was beautiful and she wanted to replicate beauty with him, have children of music, even if some of them were misshapen, unintelligible, even though she was mostly a sculptor and her blood knew mainly stone.

Today is when he returns, arrives in her again like a warmth that sinks instantly within her veins, trembles as water replacing sand before all their castles slide down, architecture abandoned to tragedy.

"James," she calls out, whispers more likely, but not without an urgency, as if she has to test how loyal he is from beyond the grave, "are you there?"

Her patio over the Delphic River is plush in this season with delphiniums, roses, Michaelmas daisies, reddening tomatoes and wasps attending each leaf and bloom. There is no wind and then there are breezes.

Or she will lie in bed at night and she and Michael are statues now.

"You are carved from marble," he says to her one evening.

"Is this a compliment?" Emily, propped on one elbow, gazing at him.

He won't look at her.

Doesn't speak again.

Once he told her she is a mannequin; another time the fulfillment of that hope in the Anne Wilkinson poem: "I'd love this body more if graved in rigid wood, it could not move."

"So I am immovable?" She is always pushing him to admit, to enlarge.

"Basically."

"From what?"

"Your grief, of course. You have made a sculpture from it and now… you are becoming it, like Ovid's women metamorphosing themselves or some nightmare from Cocteau."

"O thanks."

"I continue to love you but I don't know you anymore though oddly perhaps because I know you so well."

Michael could be annoyingly cryptic, a bitter cynic, a rational blandness.

After James died, Emily had allowed Michael to find her, the failed heroine sobbing in the dark forest, lost, because the prince had been killed but also from some even deeper murder, a collision of childhood and the first terrible time she had been made love to (how close it was to hate) and all the years she had to fend off taunts and the houses that had slipped through her arms to shatter their glass dreams on the asphalt of her mind.

But it is Sunday now and she is alone and trying to work.

Only every face her fingers form are his: sulky, impassioned, weary, devoted, the eyes always haunted by a knowledge he couldn't have known.

Emily used to say she would die before James. Then he was hit by that train he wouldn't have seen coming as he walked down the tracks in Carcassonne where he was on tour with his ode to Poe.

No one had been with him.

But the music in his head.

It was the indifference that perhaps exists at the heart of a love that must remain inaccessible.

This is what she tells Michael. When someone who loves you utterly dies, there is this sudden rupture, this unbridgeable chasm between their giving and giving while alive and then, dead, their inaccessibility, so cruel, which reads like brute indifference, a coldness to the cutting off and its aftermath and thus, this unquenchability.

When she and Michael are reclining in bed like the sarcophagi they have become and she asks silently for James to hold her, to be with her now, and for a moment she convinces herself he hears, he visits, in the next she realizes it is her imagination, or possibly a sleep paralysis that gives her the sense arms are enclosing her body, that she has fooled herself again.

But it is still Sunday now. Emily sips her coffee. The raven-furred cat slathers itself in sunshine. All about the room (she knows Michael will despair when he returns) are unfinished but wholly recognizable effigies of her ghost composer's face.

Intermission

How fitting he died after composing the ode, this final act a testimony to the artist's truth that practice never ends and techniques are always discoverable. "Dark Night" was James's ballet of the hands, a pre-elegy to the Evermore he would be for her and an homage to the poem that had marked his emergence from the sunny emptiness of childhood's sense of time into the bong-bong that the adult clock uttered with its shadowy language of words—grim, ungainly, ghastly, ominous, gaunt—as an adolescent he would lie in the post-dusk of his room repeating these adjectives like counting difficult sheep and then he would sleep sleekly in them, their hard syllables a kind of solace as if, in accepting them into him he was preparing himself for the worst, acolyte to the inevitable.

"Can I call you Lenore?" he had asked her early on in their relationship.

"Why? That's stupid, James, I'm not lost, ineffable. You're so romantically weird."

"Yeah and? Just once in a while?"

"Geez, ok. If it means that much to you!"

"It's like the terror of honey on my tongue, sweetheart."

"O darling, how *your darkness is your beauty.*"

"Come on, now who's being mushy!"

She couldn't stop recalling him to her, in *revolt against all things that die.*

Had he not told her—I will never leave you, I will be yours forever!

This was her battle and how much energy did it consume?

An excess.

She was rendered fragile by it, leaning on Michael's arm, pressing her wet face into his shoulder, waking again weeping, then once more, exhausted.

He still insisted he loved her despite this incessant donning of armour to wage a war against what can never be felled, not even by art.

James was her spectral liege, Michael knew this, couldn't forget it for an instant as wasn't that Emily again on her knees before his altar, the attar of his music opening her lips.

Monday

On the train heading to Montreal, Emily and Michael, consoled momentarily by the tiny bottles of wine, the packaged sandwiches and the very rhythms of the journey. Michael didn't act anymore but sometimes he wrote poems, short essays, small dreamings, and one of these, "Andante & Verdigris," a poem about two horses he had ridden as a boy, had won a contest and they were travelling to receive his prize, dine, be feted in the minor key as James would have said, of the rewards bequeathed to the arts in their winter country.

"You know all loss is composite." Emily had to pierce their gentle silence with another of her harsh utterances about grief, the thesis of her night.

"Mmmhmmmm." Michael crunched a salty chip, took a swift sip of the chardonnay.

"I think that's what makes aging tough to bear, beyond the physical ailments, is that accumulation."

"Are you thinking of Frank?"

"Of course, in part, I mean he did live and die at our destination. So how could I not be thinking about him. And though losing James in a sense superseded Frank's loss, in another there is no hierarchy in the realms of death and both their faces are compacted into one agitated neutron ball, shivering and gyrating and spitting out sparks of memory."

"You are so complicated."

"What do you mean?"

"Your mind doesn't rest. Even when you sleep you are teeming with analogies."

"O *love knows nothing.*"

"How can you say that?"

"Ok then, you don't love me. Thus you can coldly analyze, pick at my nightmares like the Japanese do with the bones of their dead, plucking forth the reasons."

Years before James had died, Frank, struggling with schizophrenia, had hanged himself in his bedroom with one of his father's belts. His father, a dealer. He had been a writer, of just one unfinishable novel, and his suicide note stole from Father Time in *Jude the Obscure*, scrawling as he had, "Done because we are too menny."

The menny though were not children, but voices, the polyphony of despair in his head.

Back when they were in their early twenties, they had met on this same train. He had helped her with her luggage, that massive pack she dragged about then as if she was always running away from home.

"Hey thanks," she had replied, barely able to glance at his eyes which held the whole tragic sea in them.

"I'm Frank, not Francis, but... whatever," sticking out a hand that was callused, his hair scrubbed upwards. And she didn't go where she had planned but exited instead at Dorval and was consumed inside his life for the more beautiful, ruthless part of a year.

"Are you trapped in the past again?" Michael was bumping against her, a lifeboat nudging the giant yacht of her nostalgia.

"Trapped? No, just visiting for a time."

"Good," he breathed deeply, "Only checking."

And the train continued its black progression through the pale and meltable landscapes, whipping past the couple who were really a multitude beneath the X-ray of longing.

Montreal

Is her name a magic charm?

Emily. Emily.

Michael whispers it to himself sometimes when he grows anxious as if it will protect him, those three lyrical syllables, or as if their bond will strengthen because he can utter her name after all and James, the ghost, cannot.

He doesn't know even what to think about James's magnum opus "Evermore:" is it brilliant or flawed with its pale strainings towards melodrama he senses inhabited the man like effete maggots.

Or is he jealous? His plays, his poems, even "Andante & Verdigris" are not likely to reach the kinds of audiences James had, he limited by genre, by his diminished charisma.

Michael is preparing for the awards ceremony in their softly appointed room off St. Catherines. Emily is staring out the window at the cathedral or the porn store and what is she thinking about? Her spectre again? He suspects her always of this.

"No, I am thinking about the sculpture I made last week," she replies to his suspicions lodged in the silence between them.

"But it was of him no?"

"Somewhat... perhaps."

"So you were thinking of him then."

"No Michael! I am making art. This transcends any human limitation, personal grief."

"I don't agree. It isn't possible."

"You aren't a real artist if you believe this."

"O you and your pronouncements!"

"But they are true and anyway, I need a stance against loss."

He saw her always as garlanded with memory, only the flowers were heavy and dark and she denies this, skipping and dancing before him despite this obvious burden. He feels so tired today of her inability to be exclusive, to have eternally, an other, in the past, before Frank, then James, it could have been living others, but these were easier to absorb, he is certain, they had fractures, finalities, their glass castles could be smashed.

The dead lovers?

No, they were invincible, immutable, perhaps not perfect but horribly, even their flaws were adored because they couldn't, again, harm, and so they took on the glow of the heart's idealizing museum. There is my former pain and there the disaster like shrunken heads in alarmed cases, the agony long dwindled inside the hot sand time is.

Only an hour until the ceremony and he wanted to be held awhile in Emily's mind, usurp James. If he could scour him out tonight, he would.

"Emily, *one man loves you and that man is I. Silence within!*"

She startles at his voice, turning slow from the window at this sharpness and there is both guilt in her tone and resentment.

"Michael, don't diminish love to the flesh. And I know, I know. And there is already so very much quiet at the core of everything."

Again she had left him with no way to respond and so they descended the faded staircase to the lobby without touching.

Monday Night

"And his eyes have all the seeming of a demon's that is dreaming" James used to recite as she woke, immersed in Poe as his composition unfolded, the étude was only the beginning, perhaps it would have become a whole symphony...

But no, she couldn't think like that, couldn't keep existing in the what ifs of everything, it was too terrible and besides, she is supposed to be present for Michael now, in his trembling hour of triumph—

There, his name is read out, the applause, she is standing too, he is heading up to the podium to receive his accolades, his recitation will be sonorous but possibly lacking something, a wildness, a ballast.

Emily doesn't know. Or maybe she isn't really listening after all but floating above the banquet hall in downtown Montreal on this Monday evening.

"Go on loving death," he had yelled at her earlier, *"death can never do you harm, right?"*

No, there was nothing active about the wounding of mortality; it was a passive predator she continued to beckon, to insist she be bitten over and over again in a way James never would have wanted.

Yet you lodged that word in me, didn't you, she rages privately at him, that Nevermore you have enacted, concealed yourself behind, forever.

And now Michael has his hand pressed to her shoulder, he is grinning down at her, though he is *forced to go on waiting and waiting...*

"Please forgive me," she says.

"Why?"

"You know, and… congratulations."

The champagne like springtime in their glasses and Emily pressing herself towards the present where she now must live.

Tuesday—Toronto

Tell me who you have chosen—the flames or me—Michael, was it he who woke crying this out? They were in a hotel by Kensington Market on their stopover. They had planned to return but were finding no direct route, no quick trajectory back home.

O Emily, why can't you decide?

This is the problem with the dead, she thinks, they nullify decision-making. You cannot choose to not love them anymore. They are in the record caught on the groove, the scratch where Callas is trilling "L'amour!" or "Amore" and there is no way to return the needle to the start.

Emily had dreamed of James again last night.

Even as she lay beside Michael after the hour of his victory, she was not present, never in the burning cathedrals and seared flesh of her nightmares.

They had been face to face:

"Lenny," his nickname for her, "Lenny," he had said softly, "I miss you."

And her fingers had touched his cheek, recalling how thick and comforting his skin had always seemed, forgetting, in the dark, how fast it had turned to ashes.

She had woken angry at being forever denied this intimacy and the gift of Michael then appeared as affront, everything about him so different from James as if each characteristic (hair, tone of voice, occupation, tastes,

143

shape) was annihilating all that James had been until she could claim him nowhere but in the stupid futility of her subconscious.

"You are not enough!" she wanted to scream at his sleeping body. "You never will be!"

But she knew how unfair this was and that, in the end, it had nothing to do with Michael at all, her unquenching rage, and so she fell hushed inside and waited for the sun to fall upon the linen and tiles and wood and carve a kind of peace between them.

Tuesday Night

Dearest James—is how Emily would have started this letter to the dead, or Beloved or Darling or with one of the nicknames she had for you—Sweet Puppy, Dark Elf—

But Michael begins—Dear James of the Beyond Us—if you can hear this plea I beseech you (there is always something archaic about speaking to the dead), depart—leave Emily to be mine now—not in crass ownership but simply in the solitude of two that love seeks, a relation not constantly imperilled by the fissures of what was and can be no more—you recall your adored raven—Nevermore, Nevermore, remember—that is the word imprinted on the endless void between you and Emily now—

O do you hear? You *everywhere and in everything?*

I imagine what she was before you and she must have been more wonderful to love—less fractured by regret and that sense of incompletion you have left her in where she is always an abyss, teetering on the rim of itself—she couldn't see angels nor devils in all the graveyards and cathedrals we walked without seeing you first—you the marble pinion, you the cast-down Lucifer, even, on the cross, you the ectomorphic beauty she could no longer assuage nor torture unwittingly—

It was on Monday, after my ceremony, the small award I received for the one poem—Oh, nothing like your symphonies—that it struck me—she will never be free of you with any kind of permanence and this knowledge plundered me with agony.

I cannot abide it, James. You will have to leave us, immortal and ruined singer—my poems, she knows, are instant dust and even her sculptures crumble in her perspiring hands as she cannot claim the concentration required to make them eternal—but your études are not only music; they are the pathways of your blood—they keep tracing a road back to you as if you are never anything other than fully alive or just hiding, hiding for an instant or an endlessness like the child you remain.

It is she and I, James, who have recognized each other since the beginning, within both the magic and the quotidian while you had only the dream—fleeting and a wound.

I have tried to expel you from us with verse, as every poet believes in some sense they are sorcerers and can drive away hauntings—

Dark one, unheld by time, *you do not know who my love is.* Death has left you incapable of access though, between worlds, you cling to the illusion. Let the past in us be gone because we cannot change it and so within it, we are stone when we need to be water, flooding the channels of each other above the slightest ghost diverting us into the lost salt once again.

Emily loved that poem, James—and so it is not only your art she attends—I am no mere spectre of you—at least I know this—but my own fleshed presence, and she does not find you there—I see her coming towards me now as I write you and we will walk into the stippled streets, browse in one of the market stores or another, sip coffee, then wine at small neighbourhood establishments, late, lie between sheets gentling each other—

You cannot do this anymore with her, do you hear?

So let me have that right and fall away from the night that you have become—

With gratitude, despair, hope—Michael, the weary lover.

Wednesday—St. James Cathedral

"This consecration. As if a place of worship was made from the long a of his name, Michael."

Don't be stupid is what he wants to say but instead utters—"you invest his name with too much at times, Emily; he was just a man, like me. If I died…"

But here he fades off because he knows there is not this type of bond between them, that the connection is one of life: its croissants and bus tickets, its washcloths and library books, its spats over laundry and its quick quotidian eroticisms—

If he died…

Emily wouldn't forget, no, but neither would she mould his lineaments in marble nor find him in dream, nor moan about his vanished name "nameless here forevermore" while wandering beneath the opulent nave of St. James with its explosively hued stained glass, its glowing organ and cloud-piercing spire.

No, she would hold a tastefully presentable funeral and perhaps invoke him in letters, emails. Would she wail for him at all, never mind for years?

He has to stop thinking like this, pointless as it is, damaging even.

"Emily."

"Yes."

"You know how much I love you?"

"I think so, but why must you..."

"Say it now?"

"Yes, why. It's like you fear. I feel you running towards me from a sharpening distance with these words of love your hopeful banner—will she see me, will she see me, you ask in terror."

"Is that how I appear to you?"

"O Michael, just for now can we be in the present, contained in this old wood and incense and all the candles shuddering behind red glass? I want to stop thinking about everything for a while. Especially human love, its sorrows."

"Remember what the writer said, how the dead who just lie there are the hardest to escape from."

"Yes or something like that. Why does his name have to be everywhere?"

"And yet I cannot negotiate with it anymore."

My desire is that your body shall forget nothing.

"Is this what his ghost says to me over and over?"

"Do ghosts desire still?"

They are silent then and the musk of the great church settles upon them, the ancient builders who never witnessed the completion of their vision cry out inside them—what about us? What of our long and futile labour to make what we could never enter? Is it enough you are reaping our harvest of eternity?

And now mass is about to begin. Bells ring out from the tower, echoes storming their hearts. Yet the faith they were raised in had fallen from them long ago. So they leave by the massive doorway, fingers dry of the blessed water lying still in its stone hollow.

Moment Two

Cantabile e Furioso

She woke and he was holding her, his eyes with their small haunting in each of his pupils gazing down upon the forms her sleeping took.

So often she couldn't look at him now.

There were too many answers she did not possess.

"I want to kiss your lips until they are dust and mine are dust too," Michael was slurring in drowsy rapture.

Ah melodrama, o the wrongness of romanticism, she uttered within, but knowing she too fell prey to such desires and worse, with the already annulled possibilities of the dead, kept quiet.

"Each separate dying ember wrought its ghost upon the floor…" Emily kept repeating Poe's line in her head, recalling the notes that had attended each syllable, James pressing down on the keys, not only with his fingers but with his whole being it seemed—the intensity he had in bed with her—his hunger gathering into that one swollen vein in his neck as he almost refused breath while entering her tensely until the gleam of his chest was the only light and she knew she just had to glance directly into his wilderness-gaze once for them both to become violent rivulets of pleasure, doors kicked open to water—that flood loving him could be—o!

She was so torn, would she ever be satisfied again, could she ever forgive his absence?

The heart that was now damming up the tumult of her blood had slowed to this ache for invisibility, vanishing.

Thursday

Were they back in Montreal for no reason but nostalgia or had they returned to the Delphic River or were they floating, the unmoored duo within their spectral appendage, somewhere between it all still?

Perhaps they had never left the cathedral and their sculptures, poems, songs were being created there for eternity, seeds sewn inside the velvet and incensed womb of this ancient place of worship with its stained glass fragilities.

Emily recalls how, after James died, before Michael proffered his harbouring, that so many of James's friends, collaborators, had come forth to grieve with her and how fast that commiserating had slid into lust—they had all claimed—Jean Luc, Ray, Grayson, Paul—to have loved her long and only now were they able to reveal it and would she receive them?

Emily had felt her faith fall away from the sayings of men a forever time ago. She knew that who they desired was the dead and that through her flesh, they were hoping to gain knowledge, intimacy with the missing. Yet she had held some of them naked, even burningly, and imagined along with them the fleeting fantasy that it was fate, this transference.

But it did not bring James back. Of course (she shook her head again at this convulsive delirium) and within a short time, she had seen how they were pale vagrants of who he had been and she didn't want reminders, echoes.

Where are you, so unfaithful and yet so faithful, Emily?

James is repeating this to her, in dreams, when she passes by the home on 14th they lived in together and she knows this is true—she was always both—is—even now—faithful to both James and Michael and thus unfaithful and to her, whole, incapable of being other than triangle, now with its one luminescent side. How she wanted to keep him close. How she needed to drive him from her.

Her fingers were sore from moulding such recalcitrant materials and she felt sorry Michael had to return at night to this studio where everywhere rose stone and clay and marble fragments of James's face, his hands—that he had to try to write in such a place, something beyond all this, before it, write his "Andante and Verdigris" without them being riddled with the faint melodies of Poe's Opus or scarred with the dust that sprang from her ever-unfinished effigies.

"Is there a penalty more than death for having loved so much?" is what she used to ask, but now she knows there is.

There is this living on and on and always the terrible Euridice of the lover retreating and she continuing to sing from that realm of doom and ever being so very, very tired.

Thursday Night

It is raining again, a rain that doesn't know its own mind, falling now with the gentleness of a West Coast drizzle, then abrupt and drenching as a prairie downpour and finally with the eastern relentlessness Emily had come to cherish as a representation of her own grieving, attacking in spasms and then, simply carrying on, making the whole world gleam with unsettling resonance.

She was seeking Michael who had vanished into the dark streets of this nowhere place they had ended up in.

He could not endure the effigies anymore, lying everywhere, "vast and trunkless" amid the "lone and level sands" of her heart—why these lines now—they entered her, pierced and she understood them as she never had before the suffering. Yes, the suffering that marked itself on all she touched, like a grey Midas, a king not of greed but grief, and Michael, even as he ran down les rues de la ville couldn't escape it.

He still wanted to marry her, to place the sweet stamp of belonging, not ownership, on her damp forehead, her sleep-mumbling lips, that long, muscular, scar-tortured body. Wanting this made him flee because he knew he could not, wholly, marry them both and that melding with Emily as a singular fantasy of flesh and past was not possible.

She found him gasping under a street lamp, soaked and yet jubilant with this torment.

"Will you marry me?" he panted out as if it was the last question in the world, so decrepit it no longer surged anymore with hope.

"*I am going to grow old now very ardently,*" is what she says to him, as if it is reassurance that the fire in her is already subsiding, has its plan intact to become containable ashes.

The Dream

Remember the old country, Emily, you only a child and me seeing you from afar, in Cordoba or Angers, the eldest of four, walking with your parents on a Sunday, from St. Yves de Braine, your eyes so fierce beneath that pale kerchief you had covered your dark hair with and I stopped to stare at you, little more than a youth myself and was struck and held and became Dante.

That is an agony you do not know.

Having fate say so very early on that you will follow, despite, even if years upon years elapse and countries shift to provinces and time cursives our faces, in the end, I will be yours and you a tracing in me, bound regardless of fight.

But I did not notice you then. I had my own inner quest, she says, and it was not of men. Only later, as another person, almost, the bereft one, did I see you and yet still, always, *the other distance will exist as well.* I cannot help this.

Please forgive me.

If this is marriage it is not recognizable in my silences. We must reinterpret all the heart's institutions.

So you were the youngest of ten, running beside your nurse, leaving the fields on a weekday where you had been harvesting berries and yet a seriousness beset your features.

You did not see me.

So. You, the middle child of six, all alone, sitting in La Mallerquina, sipping a café cortado, quite mature though only eight or ten, your duffel coat toggled to the neck and your gloved hands folded on the glass-topped table.

O yes, I knew you in so many different guises.

No, you only dream you knew me then, in Vitry-sur-Seine, in Leon.

We never met in the old country, only in this new unsettled place where James's symphonies continue to reverberate in my ears and I can almost not attend to your singing poems and my hands keep dipping into the dust to make and make an absence.

She is touching his soaked shoulder now.

They are weeping in the redundancy of weather.

He is repeating, *the infinite distance,* I understand, I understand.

The Final Moment

Friday—Again, the Dream

She had dreamt he had finally understood, not just empathized with that core of sorrow in her but taken it within him, this knowledge, as a deeply impersonal but transformative sense of detachment and love no one could entirely ally themselves with.

Or had he dreamed, in their small room, beneath its new snow mantle, that he would always yearn, even in coming to terms with this dearth and finding a kind of peace inside its cold walls.

He pressed himself within her and they moved together in the illusion of unity for awhile. Was she there? He was rarely sure if she was palimpsesting his face with James's or turning her back to him so she could float away in her own unknown reveries. Or nothingness.

Sometimes she was there, fleetingly.

Michael and Emily, he whispered, Michael and Emily— catching sight of her as a child in the Jardin du Plantes, the exotic foliage of her clothing, her long nutmeg hair, that delicate, obsessive way she had of glancing upon flowers, like a feverish butterfly.

"I am sorry. I wasn't really there," she was telling him.

"What, now?"

"No, not that, but, at your ceremony, your reading."

"*I feel no pain,*" Michael replied, "*I feel nothing anymore.*"

"Don't say that, don't!"

Why had she not noticed him until her hour of need when his lopsided smile, sideburned cheeks, expansive hands were gifts she could have received before taking that painful host on her tongue and uttering—I am yours, ectomorphic saviour who is not.

There were never truly answers and the light slowly trailed its bright gown away from them as they lay in silent, devoted shapes.

Friday Night

When the third person is a ghost, equations are imperilled. Emily might say this to Michael with all the fiercely emphatic underlining her tiring voice could muster:

You know well enough that temptations cannot be killed but what when the temptation is for the dead, a backwards desire, deeply nostalgic, agonizing and beyond the flesh?

When the spouse, alive, becomes the temptation, dead, the ever-yearned for, the fracturer of the now?

Emily seizes the hammer and begins to batter her sculptures, all the spectres she has shaped from clay and stone fragmenting, the low room puffed with acrid dust and the floor a map of her past love's lineaments.

"Don't!" Michael is calling out but he cannot stop her hand smashing and smashing what she has made. She knows his ire is only for her destroyed art while the victory within him is this eradication of so many relics of James, shadows he woke and slept to every day, weary visitations.

Still, he can't prevent himself from crying, "We will repair this damage. This will once again be whole!"

Emily turning towards him, the hammer like a fist at her side, her aging child's face grey with rupture and ashes. "Don't you see Michael, *I like the pieces better*; they express more of what I wanted to say all along."

The Saturday

And each separate dying ember wrought its ghost upon the floor.

Emily wished she didn't keep hearing this line in her head, how pianissimo James played it, as if his fingers were snowflakes melting instantly on the tropical keys, making a gorgeous river of sound that, it seemed, would live in her always.

Now she is walking alone in these memories.

Now she is working to forget or if not forget then to place these hauntings into another strata of her being, to dig them deeper into the topography of her mind and body so she is not always torturing Michael with James, the way he surfaces here in a touch, there in a conversation or dream.

So readily does he continue to surface.

Each separate dying ember wrought its ghost.

He died so quickly and yet the moment of his death: abrupt, stupid, a reckless entry in time, carries on and on in her.

She knows she has grown dull with recounting her tale, an Ancient Mariner who tells and tells of the albatross love is.

How she regretted having loved so much! How tired she felt!

And now all she wants is quiet, a kind of peaceful decline within another man's arms, hunger a soft hum.

She would not stand on the railing again and imagine that form of willed death, the sepia currents closing over her.

It is May or it is October.

There is nothing final about this loss.

Publication Credits

"Day of the Dead" was originally published in *Lit n Image*.

"A Brief Guide to the Vocabulary of Captors" originally appeared in *The Toronto Quarterly*.

"Food I Ate with Frank" was nominated for the Matrix Magazine Lit Pop Award (Montreal) in 2008.

"360 Degrees" originally appeared in Issue 9 of *Memewar Magazine* in 2009.

The short story "Bite, Numb, Hole" was first published in Issue 2 of *Urban Graffiti* in 2011.

"The Ceremony" was shortlisted for the Writer's Union of Canada Award in 2011.

"Johnny" first appeared in Issue 28 of *Front&Centre*.

"Pollen" first appeared in Issue 62 of *Right Hand Pointing* in 2013.

"Three Sips" was originally published in the anthology *This Place a Stranger: Canadian Women Travelling Alone* (Caitlin Press, 2014).

The Author

PHOTO PAUL SATURLEY

Catherine Owen lives in New Westminster, BC. She is the author of ten collections of poetry, among them, *Designated Mourner* (ECW Press, 2014), *Trobairitz* (Anvil Press, 2012), *Seeing Lessons* (Wolsak & Wynn, 2010) and *Frenzy* (Anvil Press, 2009). Her poems are included in several recent anthologies such as *Forcefield: 77 Women Poets of BC* (Mother Tongue Publishing, 2013), *This Place a Stranger: Canadian Women Travelling Alone* (Caitlin Press, 2014) and *In Fine Form 2nd Edition* (Caitlin Press, 2016). Stories have appeared in *Urban Graffiti, Memewear Magazine, Lit N Image* (US) and *Toronto Quarterly*. Her collection of memoirs and essays is called *Catalysts: Confrontations with the Muse* (Wolsak & Wynn, 2012). *Frenzy* won the Alberta Book Prize and other collections have been nominated for a BC Book Prize, ReLit, the CBC Prize, and the George Ryga Award. In 2015, Wolsak & Wynn published her compendium on the practices of writing called *The Other 23 and a Half Hours or Everything You Wanted to Know That Your MFA Didn't Teach You*. She works in TV, plays metal bass and blogs at *Marrow Reviews*.